Impulsion

SARAH WELK BAYNUM

Impulsion

A Novel by Sarah Welk Baynum

Editor: Laurie Berglie

Cover Designer: GermanCreative on Fiverr

ISBN: 979-8-9863339-1-5

Website:

https://sarahwelkbaynumauthor.com/

Contents

Chapter One

The warm, early morning breeze blew through Emma Walker's hair as she stood in the doorway of her guesthouse at Twin Oaks Farm.

Hands wrapped around a still steaming cup of coffee, she watched the rising sun's rays shining behind the tall live oak at the edge of the farm.

This was it; the last morning she would ever wake up on this breathtaking farm. Emma knew this day was coming, but she just couldn't quite grasp the reality that it was here. This place had become her home away from home for the last six months.

"This was my decision," she thought, reminding herself that no one was forcing her from this place. It was the right decision too, of course. The opportunity Cathy had presented was too good to pass up. It far surpassed any of the offers from other farms, and how could it not? It was quite literally a dream come true to run a farm like the one Cathy planned to purchase. Emma

had tried to absorb as much knowledge from Jenn as she could since officially accepting Cathy's offer a few weeks ago.

Emma watched the sun completely rise before turning to go back inside her guesthouse.

"I better get packing," she thought. Emma was starting to regret putting it off until today. In her defense, she had been working her regular hours at Twin Oaks until moving day, which was the agreement they had made. Since the farm she would be training at didn't have any open living accommodations, Emma had spent the last few weeks looking for an apartment to live in until Cathy found and closed on a farm.

That, unfortunately, had not been as easy as she had expected and took up most of her free time when she wasn't performing her regular barn duties at Twin Oaks.

Emma spent the next few hours packing and reminiscing about the day she moved in. It was funny how even six months could change so much.

Leaving her luggage on the bed for now, Emma headed out to the barn. Valentine was scheduled to be picked up and hauled over to the new, temporary farm this evening, giving her most of the day to move her things over to her new apartment.

Sliding open the familiar barn door, she walked first over to Jimmie John's stall. The dark bay gelding had found a special place in her heart, and he would be one of the things she would miss most at Twin Oaks.

"Don't worry bud, I'll still be watching you tear up the Grand Prix ring," Emma said, running her hand up the gelding's forelock. He nudged at her chest, making her smile.

"Be a good boy for Jenn and try not to scare off your new working student, ok?" she said before giving him a final pat.

Emma said a quick goodbye to a few of her other favorite horses before making a final stop at Valentine's stall.

"I will see you soon, lady," she said, planting a kiss on her mare's velvety nose.

"I'll see you in a couple hours!" Emma called down the aisle to Mateo, who was cleaning a stall.

"See you later," he called back, still inside the stall.

Emma walked back to the guesthouse, loading up all of her luggage and the rest of her things into her trunk. Walking back inside, she set the house keys on the table like she had promised and took one more look around the room before closing the door.

Three palm trees swayed in the breeze in front of a small lake at the entrance of the apartment complex she was about to call home. It was a far cry from the views of her former guesthouse.

"This is only temporary," she thought.

Parking in front of the clubhouse, she walked into the leasing office with the necessary documents she needed to collect her new apartment keys.

"I'm Emma Walker. I'm here to move in," she told the brunette behind the desk as she handed over the paperwork and a check.

"Perfect, this is all we need. Let me grab your keys, and I will show you where your apartment is on the map. It looks like your apartment is in a great location. Lucky you!"

Emma was sure the leasing agent meant well, but compared to where she came from, she doubted it would seem "great" to her.

"*Temporary,*" she reminded herself again.

Emma thanked the young women once more as she headed back to her car with her new set of keys. Following the winding road that led to the back side of the apartment complex, she found the side street the leasing agent had pointed out on the map. Parking in front of her new apartment, she unlocked the front door and walked in.

The apartment came furnished, a must for her, and as she entered the townhome style apartment, she walked into a small dining area followed by a kitchen with white cabinetry and a faux wood vinyl floor. The kitchen was open and bordered the living room, which had a small loveseat couch that sat across from a TV on a stand, and she could see the sliding patio door at the edge of the living room. Before walking upstairs to investigate the bedroom, she slid the glass door open and stepped onto the concrete patio.

"Alright, this view isn't so bad; it's not Twin Oaks, but...," her thoughts trailed off as she stepped out onto the grass, scanning the area behind her apartment. There was a significant amount of greenspace between her patio and the glistening lake behind it. A few scattered palm trees surrounded the lake, and what appeared to be a lightly wooded area lay behind that. Sliding the patio door shut behind her after walking back inside, she headed up the stairs to the open loft style bedroom area. A queen bed with a light grey comforter and a small, dark wood nightstand was all the room had to offer, but it was all she needed.

Emma flopped lazily onto the bed, rolling over to look out the window that had a partial view of the lake. She had to admit, it was a better view than her old apartment back in Ohio. Twin Oaks' breathtaking views had spoiled her, and she was sure her home at the farm Cathy would be purchasing would be equally gorgeous.

Sighing audibly, she pushed herself off the bed and headed back to her car to unpack her things.

There was so much she had to be thankful for, and she promised herself to keep that in mind while she was in this period of limbo.

Dragging the last of her tack, tack boxes, and other items of Valentine's scattered around Twin Oaks Farm, Emma slid down the side of the barn, sitting in the grass. The hauler had called to say he was almost there, so she took the few minutes she had left to rest her tired legs. It had been a long day of unpacking at her new apartment and packing Valentine's things.

The sun hung low in the sky, and Emma soaked in the last few moments of her time here while she had them.

"*This is it,*" she thought, knowing how much she was going to miss this place.

"Do you want some help loading your tack into the trailer?" she heard Michael's voice say in the aisleway of the barn behind her.

"You know, I may just take you up on that. It's been a long day, thanks," she replied, turning around as she spoke. Emma's eyes met Michael's briefly, but she looked away, cheeks flushed, moments later.

The last few weeks since the night he kissed her at the Twin Oaks end of season party had been, well, awkward to say the least. For three straight days afterwards, they only spoke to each other when it was strictly work related. Emma remembered avoiding extended eye contact those first few days. Every time she looked at him, she felt a wave of guilt. Not that it had been her fault; Michael had kissed her after all. It was clear he felt guilty by the way he looked at her, and surely, the numerous drinks he had that night played into his impulsion.

Sure, things had improved a little since, but it was safe to say they were still finding their footing as friends again.

Neither of them had mentioned the kiss out loud to this day, and Emma had no intention of doing so. She could only hope they could go back to the way things were at some point. After all, she still wanted Michael in her life; that hadn't changed.

Emma heard the rattle of the large, empty trailer and diesel engine pulling into the driveway and stood up, brushing the grass off her jeans. Grabbing her saddle and a few other items that fit on her arm, she began loading up the hauler's trailer. Michael picked up the tack trunk and followed her to the trailer's tack room.

Emma turned around after setting her tack in the trailer, almost bumping directly into Michael, who was much closer than she realized.

"Oh...sorry," she stammered, swerving out of his way as she walked back to the barn to grab the rest of her things.

"*Yep, still awkward,*" she thought, after seeing the look on Michael's face with hers so close to his.

With the last of her things in the trailer, she headed to Valentine's stall to prep her for the short trailer ride to their new farm. Emma glanced around the now quiet barn one last time, saying a mental goodbye to this chapter in her life as it ended the moment Valentine was on that trailer. Giving Jimmie John's nose a quick pet as she walked down the aisle, she headed back towards the trailer. Once her horse was loaded, she thanked the hauler and told him she would be right behind him.

Michael and Emma turned to one another almost simultaneously, realizing this was goodbye for now. It started to sink in as they still held each other's gaze, that she wouldn't be seeing Michael everyday anymore. In fact, she didn't know the next time she would see him. Of course, Emma assumed they would make plans and see each other when they could, but that was before that night of the season end party. Once she had officially accepted Cathy's offer, Emma had mentioned it to him casually, but they had not really spent much time discussing it since.

"This could be my only chance to fix things with Michael," she thought. This awkwardness had to end now; their friendship depended on it since they would no longer be seeing each other every day by default.

Emma walked purposefully toward him, wrapping her arms around his neck before he could open his mouth to say anything. After half a second of surprise, she felt him wrap his arms around her back. Pulling away, she looked him in the eye, hoping to convey her message before saying, "Don't be a stranger, ok?"

Michael smiled at her for the first time since she could remember and said, "I'll call you tomorrow; we'll celebrate over some Mexican food and margaritas soon." She smiled back before heading quickly toward her car, hearing the truck and trailer heading toward the entrance.

"See you," Emma said, looking back it him once more before sliding into the front seat of her car.

Peering in her review mirror right before she exited the farm's black iron gates, she saw Michael standing where she left him staring at her car until it faded from view.

A sign that read "Three Phases Farm" welcomed her as she turned off a back country road and onto the long winding driveway. Emma remembered the first time she saw Ben David's farm the night of his party earlier in the year. It was twice as breathtaking today, knowing it would be her and Valentine's temporary farm home.

Recalling the conversation with Cathy two weeks ago, she remembered her presenting the options for trainers and farms.

"Alright dear, I have a few people I spoke with that have the stall space for Valentine and are willing to work with you while we look for a farm," Cathy had said. "Let's see, we have Howard Barnes, Leslie Cromm, Ben David…,"

"Ben David?! You got Ben David to agree to work with me?" Emma had said, cutting Cathy off before she could finish her list.

"Actually yes, he and I rode against each other for years, so I thought I would call in a favor. When I told him who you were, he mentioned meeting you and that you were a friend of his working student. He said he'd be happy to have you."

Emma's jaw all but hit the floor when Cathy had said that. "I want to train with Ben David; no need to go on," Emma had said excitedly, making Cathy laugh at her enthusiasm.

"Well, I guess it's settled then dear! I will give him a call and set it up."

Emma snapped back to reality as she parked behind the trailer, now stopped in front of her. Not only was she thrilled to be working with Ben David, whom she had always admired, but the bonus was that Lily was now working for Ben full-time and still planned to work for him part-time while in veterinary school. Emma had been thrilled to hear Lily planned to stay local and would be attending the University of Florida College of Veterinary Medicine in the fall.

Lily must have heard the truck and trailer rattle down the drive because she was at Emma's car window waving excitedly before she had a chance to open her door.

"Lily!" Emma exclaimed, hugging her friend tightly. She may be excited for the new farm Cathy would be purchasing, but she had to admit, working alongside Lily for however long that may be, was going to be fun.

"Em, I am so excited you're finally here. I have been counting down the days since we're officially coworkers," her friend said, grinning broadly. The two young women chatted excitedly as they headed towards the trailer where the hauler was pulling down the ramp.

Emma led her mare from the trailer, and Lily led the way into one of two barns on the property. Admiring the bright white wood barns with hunter green shutters, she felt lucky to be at a barn of such caliber. Set back on the far-left side of the main driveway, three similarly sized barns sat half an acre apart and were a short walking distance to the spacious outdoor arena to their right. To the far right of the driveway, for as far as her eye could see, were pastures with slow rolling hills.

They walked through the already open barn doors, and Emma saw that it appeared to have about fifteen or so stalls. The stalls were open-air style and had the option to close all the way, but many were open with stall guards.

Lily stopped at the last stall on the left, closest to the wash racks and grooming bays. "This one is Valentine's," Lily said, motioning to the empty stall.

Emma led her mare inside, and Valentine immediately started lipping at the flakes of hay that were already in the corner of the stall. She smiled at her mare as she hung up her stall guard; Valentine seemed completely unfazed by her new environment.

"Come on, I'll show you around," Lily said, leading the way down the barn aisle.

Emma peered into each stall as they made their way through the barn, looking at each horse and admiring how healthy and fit they were.

They stepped out of the barn, and the breeze blew Emma's hair around as she stared out at the endless rolling hills before her.

"So, this is barn one," Lily said, pointing to the barn they had just been in, "and barn two is next to it, and barn three is beside two. Over there is the outdoor arena and next to it is the dressage ring, obviously. There is a galloping path that runs almost the entire perimeter of the farm," she said.

"I can't wait to use that," Emma thought.

"There are two apartments above each of the barns, and I live above barn one still. Ben said I'm welcome to stay there until I start vet school and drop down to part-time. You should stay with me once and a while!" Lily added, giving her friend a side hug simultaneously.

"That would be so fun Lil," Emma said, leaning into her friend's embrace.

"I may not be a fan of change, and it will be tough adjusting to a new farm, but it sure will be nice to see Lily every day," she thought.

"Across the driveway to the right, as you can see, are the pastures, and tucked a little bit to the left of those behind some of those trees is the cross country course. Back further into the property is the main house, which you probably remember from the party."

Emma nodded, taking in the expansive farm; it had to be about three times larger than Twin Oaks.

"The shavings pile, manure pile, and hay shed are on the side of barn three. Every barn has its own tack room, feed room, wash stall, and grooming bays. I think that about covers it," Lily said, putting her hands on her hips as she looked around, making sure she hadn't forgotten to tell Emma anything else.

"Thanks for the tour. I don't think I realized just how big this place was until now," Emma said.

"You'll love it here, I'm sure of it. Do you want helping putting your tack away? It looks like the hauler stacked it up next to barn one," Lily said.

"Do you mind? That would be great!" Emma replied.

The two women worked together to find a place for all Emma's tack and tack box. Emma couldn't help but enjoy the quality time with her friend, even if they were just putting away tack. The sun had completely set by the time they were finished.

"Do you want to see my barn apartment before you head home?" Lily asked.

"Of course!" Emma replied.

Lily walked up the steps located at the end of the barn aisle and opened the door to her studio style apartment. The walls, floor, and ceiling were all the same wood as the interior of the barn. A bed and nightstand were on one wall and a small kitchenette was on the other. A large window ran halfway across the exterior wall.

"It's not much but...," Lily said, shrugging, trailing off.

"Lily, this place is super cozy, and probably not much smaller than my guesthouse was at Twin Oaks. Honestly, I love it."

"It is cozy. I've loved living here," Lily said, leaning against the wall. "By the way, Ben David said to say welcome and he's sorry he wasn't available to greet you when you arrived. He's coming back from a competition, but he will be here tomorrow. He's a great boss and an incredible rider; you're super lucky to be working under him!"

"I know I am," Emma said solemnly. Lucky hardly covered how she felt about this opportunity and everything Cathy had offered her.

"How are things with Liam? Is he officially living in Wellington now?"

"Yes, he moved the rest of his things from Ohio into his Aunt Cathy's as of late last week. He starts his new job working for a general contractor construction firm in Wellington tomorrow, actually."

"That's great! Have you seen him much since the night of the Million Dollar Grand Prix?"

"No, only twice. He has been bouncing back and forth between Ohio and Wellington while he was in the process of moving and interviewing for jobs, so we haven't been able to see each other much."

"Well, I'm sure now that he's settled you two will be able to spend more time together," Lily replied sympathetically.

"I hope so; it has been hard being so far apart. Anyway, I better head back so I can get a good night's sleep before tomorrow. I still need to dig all my riding gear out of my suitcases anyway," Emma said.

"Well, I will see you tomorrow, co-worker!" Lily said, wrapping her arms around her friend.

"See you tomorrow," Emma said, returning her friend's embrace before walking out of the barn apartment.

Gazing up at the stars as she trekked back to her car, Emma basked in the fact that she was luckier than she could have ever imagined.

Chapter Two

Driving down route twenty-seven first thing in the morning was something Emma had not yet experienced.

Since she always woke up on the farm and never had a reason to be out on the road so early, she had never seen just how breathtaking this highway was when morning's first light shined down on the rolling hills. It peeked out from behind large oaks with Spanish moss blowing in the light breeze, and it glimmered off the dew that still clung to the cool grass.

While she still missed waking up on a farm and hearing the horses' excited greetings first thing, she had to admit, this was a close second.

Emma parked in the small gravel lot that was parallel to the pasture fence line closest to the driveway. A buzz of nerves and excitement ran through her as she headed towards barn one. Perhaps it was that she almost didn't feel worthy of being here, or maybe it was simply first day jitters. Either way, she hoped to live up to any expectations Ben and his staff may have of her.

Lord knows Cathy probably went on and on about her, typical Cathy, but that only made the pressure of this day that much worse.

Walking through the barn doors, she was greeted by Valentine's low friendly nicker and Lily's face peering out of the grooming bay at the end of the aisle.

"Good morning!" Lily called down the aisle, setting down the brush she had been using on a flea bitten gray. She walked over to Emma, a smile plastered on her face. With Lily at her side, this first day at Three Phases Farm couldn't be so bad, right?

"Ben David is working one of his horses in the arena. He said to send you his way once you arrived," Lily said.

"Ok, so she won't exactly be right by my side," she thought.

A flutter of excitement swept over Emma again; would she ever get used to working side by side with such a talented rider and trainer?

"Thanks Lily, I'll head that way now."

Emma gave her mare a quick dose of affection as she headed out the back door of barn one towards the arena.

As Emma approached the ring, she realized just how large it actually was. Several people could be riding or jumping in this ring at the same time without a problem. Ben David was landing a chestnut gelding, whom she assumed was at least 16.3 hands, off a ramped oxer. It was the kind of oxer that would make her want to cry a little as she approached it, and if she had to guess, it was over 4ft tall. Ben, however, seemed to sail over the enormous fence like it was nothing but a cross-rail.

He must have noticed her now staring wide-eyed next to the fence surrounding the ring because he slowed the horse to a walk and headed her direction.

"Remain calm, and don't say anything stupid," she told herself.

"Hi Emma, it's nice to see you again," Ben said warmly to her.

"I can't thank you enough for this opportunity to work with you," Emma said, just glad the words came out coherently.

"Of course, Cathy Anderson is a dear old friend and has said so many good things about you," Ben replied.

"That's what I was afraid of," she thought.

"I hope I can live up to all her kind words," she replied.

"Don't worry, we will make an eventer out of you yet," Ben said, laughing warmly as he spoke.

Emma couldn't help but feel welcomed by Ben despite the fact that she was still a little starstruck. He was certainly every bit as nice and down to earth as Lily had described him.

"The gray mare named Nettie that Lily is tacking up as we speak is your first ride of the day. Don't worry, she's an old pro who knows her job well. It will be good for you to get a feel for cross country and a little bit of some beginner novice dressage on a horse who isn't quite so green," Ben said.

Emma swallowed hard; it had been a long time since she had done any kind of cross country schooling. Not that she had done a lot of it in general, but Maggie had always made it a point to take her and the other riders out at least once a year. She said it made their horses well-rounded and was good practice for some of the natural fences found on course at hunter paces. All summer long for most of her teenage years, Emma, Lily, and a few of the other girls at Maggie's barn would do a hunter pace once a month in hopes of taking the Grand Champion title in their division in the fall. The hunter paces were based on riding a set course in an optimum time and had close to thirty natural or cross country type fences that were optional to jump. Although, they were never the type of riders to pass up a jump unless the ground was exceptionally muddy around a particular fence.

Emma hoped those years of hunter paces and cross country schooling had prepared her for this moment. She heard soft footfalls behind her and turned to see Lily leading the flea bitten gray towards her.

"Guess we are about to find out," she thought, as she took the reins from Lily.

"Lily, could you please walk out Alibi for me?" Ben said, sliding off the chestnut gelding as he spoke.

"Of course! Have a good ride, Em," she said, smiling confidently at her friend as she led the gelding away.

Emma clung to Lily's good vibes as she headed towards the mounting block. She turned to the mare briefly before getting on, running her hand up her forelock as she spoke softly to her. Emma had always had a special place in her heart for mares and felt it was a bit of good luck that her first ride at this new farm was on one. She never quite understood the negativity so many horse people had toward them. Sure, they could be a little harder to connect with at first, but she found with some finesse and treating them like a partner and not a machine that they had more heart than most geldings she had ridden.

Swinging her leg over, she sat softly in the saddle and gave the mare a gentle squeeze, asking her to walk forward.

"All right Emma let's just work on warming you both up and focus on getting to know how she rides. This one is incredibly sensitive, so a little bit of aid go a long way with her."

Her own mare was the same, sensitive to her every aid and every little change in her seat, so she couldn't help but be grateful this mare was a similar ride.

Trotting now, she couldn't help but notice this mare had a bit more bounce to her step than Valentine's silky-smooth gaits. Not that she minded, her time riding Jimmie John and the other young, green horses at Twin Oaks had prepared her to ride just about anything.

Emma asked the mare to canter after they were warmed up at the trot, noticing this gait was just as bouncy but a little more comfortable than she expected.

Ben spent fifteen minutes going over some dressage seat position basics with her, and Nettie responded to Emma's every request with ease. She certainly was an old pro, and Emma felt her body relaxing with each passing minute.

"Let's go ahead and jump a few things here in the ring first before we head out to cross country," he said, motioning towards the low vertical jump on the quarter line.

Emma forced her mind to focus on the jump ahead of her, despite it wanting to wander to the fact that a four-star eventer was about to watch her jump one of his horses for the first time. It made her feel a vulnerability in her riding she hadn't even felt the first time she rode in front of Jenn at Twin Oaks. Sure, she had been a little nervous about that, but it was nothing compared to this.

Counting strides in her mind, she felt each stride the mare took under her, looking past the jump like she had always been taught. Nettie jumped it casually, landing in a nice rhythm as she looked for her next fence.

"Yep, total pro," she thought.

"Nice Emma, go ahead and circle, take that vertical again then take that oxer on the diagonal," Ben called out from across the ring, pointing towards her next jump.

Emma turned her body towards the oxer after landing the vertical a second time. It appeared to be close to three foot, which normally didn't faze her on her own horse, but felt somehow more intimidating on a horse she had never ridden before.

Focusing on the jump ahead of her once more, she sat up tall and legged the mare up to the ramped oxer. Nettie took a deep spot, tucking her legs under her, and cleared the jump by half an inch, landing and cantering off at a nice on course pace.

With that, any fear she started with melted away. This was a nice horse, and she felt an instant connection with the way she liked to be ridden, more than likely because it was so close to how she rode Valentine.

"That looked great; she seems to like you! Let's head out to cross country," Ben said, opening the gate to the arena. Ben followed behind her as she rode Nettie through the open grassy area in between the arena and the cross country course.

Since the cross country course was settled at the base of a hill making it hard to see from the barns, this was the first time she laid eyes on it; it did not disappoint.

About twenty-five or so cross country jumps of various heights and styles lay widely-scattered across the open valley. Here and there a few live oaks dotted the field, providing a little shade to some parts of the area. And just when she thought the farm couldn't be any more breathtaking!

"There is a small table to the far left and a brush box about ten strides past that. Go ahead and take those and we will see how you do. Remember, this isn't stadium jumping; you want a nice forward pace, and you want to let her take them out of stride. Just look for the distance, and she will show you how it's done," Ben said, interrupting her gawking at the impressive course.

Emma nodded, asking Nettie to canter forward. Sitting up in a soft half seat like Maggie had taught her, she focused on finding her rhythm as they headed across the field towards the beginner novice sized table.

Counting aloud, Emma felt the mare's hooves leave the ground, picking a slightly different take off distance than she originally saw.

"Let her take it out of stride," Ben's words rang in her mind; she was still seeing show jumping distances.

The brush box ahead of her was a little larger, maybe novice level height if she had to guess. Emma focused on seeing a similar distance to the one Nettie took last time, keeping the mare forward and in front of her leg.

This time, she felt in sync with the horse as she took the brush box perfectly out of stride.

"Much nicer that second time; that's how you want to take every cross country fence," Ben said when they reached him again. After another ten fences, Emma felt her confidence grow with each jump. It had been so long that she had almost forgotten the magic of galloping around a cross country course. As much as she loved show jumping, she couldn't help but feel like this was where she truly belonged.

"Great job today! Go ahead and walk Nettie out. Lily has a list of the horses you will be exercising after you've cold hosed Nettie. They will just need some schooling on the flat, and a few on that list will be marked and can be jumped over small stadium fences as well," Ben said before heading back towards the barns.

Emma figured this would be a good time to familiarize herself with the grounds while walking this mare out. After all, scenic walks on her horse, or the horses she worked, had always been her favorite thing to do at Twin Oaks.

Loosening her reins so Nettie could walk long and low, she headed towards the galloping path that Lily had mentioned ran the perimeter of the property. This was one of the things she had been the most excited to explore since arriving here, and thus far, she was not disappointed. In many ways, this farm reminded her of a much larger version of Twin Oaks. It made sense too, since she was only about ten minutes from her former farm and the terrain was nearly identical.

At one point, she had to turn around and head back to the barns since there was simply too many acres of land and Nettie was more than walked out now.

"Not a bad problem to have," she thought.

Lily was wrapping the legs of one of the horses Ben had since ridden when she returned to the barns.

"How did it go?" Lily asked, peering out from behind the horse's leg.

"You were right; Ben is the best, and so down to earth," Emma said, pulling the tack off Nettie. Emma gave Lily the play by play of her ride as she finished untacking the mare.

"Alright, show me this list. I'm ready to ride some new horses," Emma said, her excitement now outweighed the last glimmer of anxiety about her first day here. There was something about riding a new horse for the very first time. To Emma, it was an emotional and magical experience to connect with a horse on that level. It was both challenging and exciting at the same time.

Lily pulled a crinkled paper from the pocket of her breeches, holding it up so Emma could see.

"Looks like you have four more horses to ride today. Ben is clearly going easy on you for your first day," she said, winking at her friend.

"Let's see, the first two are flat only, those are pretty young, green ones, so that makes sense. The last two are a little more experienced, I think going novice at competition and schooling training, but still fairly young," Lily added.

Emma quizzed Lily a little longer about each horse, hoping to get an idea about their personalities and way of going before getting on them. Within the hour, the first horse on Lily's list was in the cross ties tacked up and ready to go.

"Oh, I almost forgot, before you ride, I'm supposed to introduce you to some of the other staff," Lily said, leading her out of barn one and towards the other two.

"All of the horses in barn one are Ben's, and of course our horses are in barn one. About half of barn two is his horses too, and the other half is syndicate horses he's a partial owner in. Barn three is all boarders or horses he owns but are retired. Barn one is always the first one they do when they clean stalls so odds are they will be done or wrapping up with stall cleaning and such when you get here in the morning," Lily said as they walked into barn three.

"Guys, this is Emma; she will be riding with Ben for a while."

Two of the men were in the respective stalls and peeked their heads out to give a friendly wave or hello.

"That's Don and Hank," Lily said, pointing each out as she spoke. "Luis is the one grooming that bay gelding and dumping water buckets just outside the door there is Clint, who actually just started with us today as well," Lily added.

"Nice to meet all of you," Emma said as they walked out of barn three and into barn two.

"Oh good, glad we caught you before you rode. Emma, this is Ben David's head trainer and barn manager, Julia."

"Welcome Emma! I have been looking forward to meeting you," Julia said, reaching out to take her hand. Julia was tall and thin with dirty blonde hair that peeked out of the sides of her helmet.

"So nice to meet you, Julia! I'm looking forward to working with you as well," Emma replied to the young woman. Lily had always said the nicest things about Julia, and she was hoping to siphon all the knowledge she could from her before becoming a barn manager herself.

The rest of the day flew by after that, as it always seemed to at Twin Oaks when she was exercising horses. Slumped on the side of the barn as she chugged the last of her water, Emma thought about the events of the last few days.

While she still missed certain things about Twin Oaks, namely Michael and her former guesthouse, she felt an assurance about her decision to leave now that her first day at Three Phases was just about over.

Sliding her phone from her pocket, she dialed Michael's number; he had called halfway through her last ride, but she had been unable to answer.

"How was your first day on the new farm?" Michael asked on the other line. Emma filled him in, and Michael chimed in with more questions as she spoke.

"If you want, I could pick you up at the farm, and we could go to dinner?" he asked.

"That would be great! I still haven't had time to grocery shop for the new apartment anyway," Emma replied.

"I'll be there in twenty minutes," Michael said before he hung up.

Emma smiled as she put her phone away. It seemed like maybe the friendship between them was starting to rekindle despite her original concerns after all.

ele

Emma and Lily were sitting in the grass near the farm's parking lot when Michael pulled in the driveway in the Twin Oaks truck.

As his boots hit the gravel, Emma watched the look on his face as he scanned the expansive grounds. It was probably a similar look to the one she had her first day here as well.

"This place is...," Michael said, his voice trailing off.

"I know," Emma said in a soft voice, standing next to him now.

"Nice seeing you, Michael. Have a good night, Em!" Lily said, waving as she headed back to her barn apartment.

Alone now, Emma couldn't help but feel a little bit awkward around Michael still. Sure, talking on the phone was one thing. But in person, there was still something a little off between them.

"Want to say hi to Valentine and see the other side of the property?" Emma asked, hoping a little walk around the farm would help before they were stuck at a table together where the awkwardness would only be intensified.

"Sure," he replied, following behind her as she led him into barn one. Valentine greeted her human friend, nudging his pockets for the treats he typically brought her.

"I see someone hasn't forgotten me yet," Michael said, scratching the mare in her favorite place as he pulled a treat from his pocket.

"You know, it could just be that you always carry treats around with you," Emma teased.

"You never know when you will need horse bribery," Michael replied, shoulders shrugging for a moment before handing the mare another snack.

As her horse happily crunched on the treat, he walked across the aisle to pet some of the other horses whose heads hung out of their stalls, now suddenly interested in his presence.

Emma watched as he greeted several other horses who were wide-eyed and hoping for a treat of their own. Staring at him walking the aisles of this strange new barn, she found herself remembering that day he taught her to drive the trailer, the day that had truly solidified their friendship.

It was their shared love of horses that had brought them together, and she hoped it would be the glue that held them now, despite any awkwardness.

Chapter Three

If there was one thing Emma loved most about working at horse farms, besides her actual work, it was the quiet evenings she spent with Valentine after the day was done and the farm was all but abandoned.

It was as if, for that hour or so, this incredible property was all hers. Emma kept her habit of evening rides at this new farm, and this evening's weather was proving to be just about perfect.

Valentine galloped across the grass, ears pricked, as Emma pointed her towards a small chevron jump at the edge of the cross country course.

Two weeks at Three Phases Farm and she felt like she was already gaining some confidence both in the dressage arena and on the cross country course. Valentine had exceeded her expectations when it came to cross country. Although, could she really be all that surprised? There was nothing this mare loved more than galloping and jumping, no matter what form those jumps came in.

Dressage, however, was proving to be a challenge with the little chestnut. This was certainly a phase Emma expected to come with its set of challenges though, and with time and patience, she was sure her mare would understand what was being asked of her.

For now, Valentine was simply happy to be soaring over solid objects, happy as could be that it was jumping day.

Turning her head, Emma pointed the mare in the other direction towards the water. While jumping anything on cross country was no big deal, her mare had decided that any water she couldn't see to the bottom of couldn't be trusted. Could she really blame her horse though? Mares seemed to have that extra sense of self-preservation, and Valentine was no exception. It had taken almost a full week before her horse would trot through the water complex without refusing. Today, she decided to try her luck at the canter.

Emma legged the mare on, feeling her beginning to suck back at the sight of the water. Breaking to a trot two strides before the water, Valentine trotted through it, still making sure her owner knew she wasn't thrilled about it.

Laughing while rolling her eyes, Emma patted the mare for her efforts anyway.

"Some things take longer than others," she thought.

Breaking to a walk when they reached the entrance of one of the largest pastures on the property, she walked her mare through as they began their walking out ritual amongst the scattered live oaks the pastures provided.

Halfway through their cooling session, she felt her phone buzz in her pocket.

"Liam! So you are alive," she teased, answering the phone.

Unfortunately for her, Liam's new job had been proving to be busier than he'd expected. Every time they spoke on the phone, which was about once a day in the evenings or mornings before work, he seemed to be apologizing for the cutting the conversation short. Meetings, another call, or an inspection at a job site seemed to be his typical list of reasons. Not that she hadn't been busy herself, of course. Emma may not be a working student anymore, but her days were still long and busy.

"I know, I'm sorry. I know I said I would call you back this morning after I had to take that other call, but by the time I got off the phone I was at the job site," Liam said.

"Typical," she thought.

"I have some news though that will hopefully make up for that. There is this charity event Aunt Cathy is a part of, and we would love for you come down to Wellington Friday through Sunday this weekend. I know we haven't seen each other in a while, so we can spend some time together before and after the event. What do you say?" Liam asked.

"This weekend? I'll have to run it past Ben. I get weekends off but not usually Friday. I'm sure it will be fine though; I can maybe offer to work next Saturday instead. Tell Aunt Cathy I'll be there," Emma replied.

"Great, Em! I promise things will get better soon. I'll see you Friday," Liam said, before hanging up.

"It would be nice to see Liam and visit Wellington," she thought.

Luckily, enough time had passed that she didn't feel any resentment toward the city simply because it was where she had her traumatic event of being stalked. For the most part, she had put that behind her.

It was hard to believe she hadn't seen Liam in three weeks now, and she was eager to spend time with him and really catch him up on how things were going for her at Ben David's farm. Emma supposed she should tell Michael she was going to Wellington for the weekend. After all, that's what friends do, right?

They still talked every few days, but she hadn't seen him since her first night at this farm. Oddly enough, they had made plans to go to the local racetrack soon. It was almost embarrassing that she hadn't watched any live horse races since arriving in Ocala, and Michael had happily volunteered to go with her. Back home, the local racetrack had closed a few years before she left to come to Florida. Emma remembered going with Maggie several times to bring horses home that were desperate for a place to land after retiring since owners and trainers were scrambling to sell them. It was actually the way Lily found her horse, Annie. That was the last time Emma had been to a racetrack, and felt she was long overdue.

There was only one problem with this little trip to Wellington. The few times she had seen Liam after Michael kissed her, she had not mentioned Liam's visits to him. Liam had driven to see her, and it was always on her day off. She and Michael weren't talking much then anyway, so it was never something Emma felt she needed to tell Michael. This, however, was a different story. They were on their way to recovering the friendship they once had, before the kiss, and she would be gone for three days out of town. It was certainly something she couldn't avoid telling him.

So, Emma decided she would talk to Michael about this trip in person at the track tomorrow. Dread was already washing over her at the thought of that conversation. The last thing she wanted to do was take their friendship two steps back, but what choice did she have?

Liam still didn't know about the kiss and Emma didn't plan to tell him. She had thought long and hard about it afterwards but found no reason to bring it up to Liam. Michael had immediately said he regretted it, and nothing but awkwardness had followed anyway. Telling Liam would only upset him, and possibly worse, make him hate Michael for it. The last thing Emma wanted was to have to choose between her relationship with Liam and her friendship with Michael.

If given the choice at this very moment, she wasn't even sure what she would choose.

Sighing heavily as she pushed the stressful thoughts from her head, Emma focused on the few minutes she had left of her ride and the gorgeous views of this farm.

Her mare's ears swiveled as she took in the scenery as well, her hooves falling softly on thick late spring grass.

She would just have to worry about tomorrow's problems tomorrow.

Emma could feel the energy coming off the racetrack the moment she stepped into the parking lot. Michael looked over at her 'kid on Christmas morning' expression and smiled. She was glad he understood her horse obsession, because being at the track, or even horse shows for that matter, always seemed to bring it out.

While she loved watching the actual race, one of her favorite things to do was go to the backside of the track and watch the bustling activity of the grooms, riders, and horses. Thanks to Cathy's connections, they were equipped with all access passes.

Strolling down the backside, Emma's face lit up with each sleek Thoroughbred athlete that passed in colorful racing silks. It had certainly been far too long since she had been to the races. They found a bench to sit on that was close enough to watch the horses being saddled and paraded until it was time to find their actual seats.

"Michael, there's something I want to talk to you about, and I'm not going to lie, it's going to be awkward, because of, well…," she trailed off, searching his face in hopes he understood what she was trying to communicate without having to say it.

"I'm a big boy, Em. Whatever it is, I can handle it," he said, locking eyes with her beneath his ball cap.

"Well, I'm going to see Liam and Cathy this weekend in Wellington. I know you're not stupid, and that you know I've seen him since…since we…," Emma stammered.

"Just say it, Em. I kissed you. I'm not proud of it, I had no right kissing you knowing you were with Liam. It happened, but you aren't going to hurt my feelings by saying it." Michael said, still holding her gaze.

This would have been the perfect moment for Emma to ask Michael why he did it. Sure, he had been drinking, but was it truly a mistake, or was it that he had the nerve to do so because of alcohol?

Asking him now might mean she would get an answer she couldn't un-hear. One that would change everything between them. That was something she simply couldn't risk.

"Yes, er, the kiss," Emma said, her cheeks flushing red as she said it aloud. "I just wanted you to know where I would be...," she said, letting her words trail off. They both fell silent for a minute, neither looking at each other. At least, she assumed he wasn't looking at her. Biting her lip, she stared at the horses parading in front of her instead.

"Did I tell you I have my first eventing competition scheduled for two weeks from this weekend?" she asked, finally breaking the silence.

"It was most definitely time to change the subject," she thought.

"What horses are you bringing?" Michael asked, his voice casual like the awkward conversation from several minutes ago never existed. Emma supposed that was what she wanted, right?

"Ben wants me to ride his experienced horse, Nettie, at novice level, one of the younger project horses at beginner novice, and I think I'm going to bring Valentine for fun to see how she does just at beginner novice," Emma replied.

"I'm glad you're able to bring Valentine too. Are you nervous about competing in eventing for the first time?" Michael asked.

"A little," she admitted with a shrug. "But I'm excited too. The thought of galloping a cross country course that's not the one on the farm has me more excited than nervous. Although, I am a little worried about my dressage phase, especially with Valentine. She loathes dressage," Emma added, rolling her eyes.

"I could see that," Michael said with a chuckle.

"I'd love for you to come, if you want," she said, turning to meet his eyes as she did.

"Of course, I would love to come support you," Michael replied.

"Great!" she said, smiling warmly at him. "Ready to find our seats?"

"Sure," he said, standing up.

Walking side by side towards the seated area of the track, she couldn't help but think she saw a strange look on Michael's face. Perhaps their earlier conversation had affected him more than he let on.

Reminding herself it was best not to know the answer to that question, she focused her attention back on the track ahead of them.

"And they're off!" The announcer's voice echoed minutes later. Thoroughbreds with bulging muscles powered down the track flinging up chucks of dirt as they tore around the turn.

Emma wondered what it would be like to be aboard one of these incredible athletes during a race. Sure, she had galloped off-the-track Thoroughbreds in fields many times, but that didn't hold a candle to something like this. Maybe this was why she loved cross country so much, the feel of that power under her as they galloped into open space, there was absolutely nothing like it in the world.

Honestly, she wished she had switched to eventing years ago when Maggie had started taking some of her other riders to eventing trials.

"Better late than never," she thought.

It made sense why Cathy wanted to get back to her roots of eventing, even if she wasn't the one aboard the horse. Even in the few weeks of schooling she had been doing with Valentine, she noticed a significant change in her mare's use of her body, compliments of the dressage training. The bond she felt between them on cross country surpassed even what she felt on course during show jumping, which was not something she had expected.

"It's Flyby's Legacy by two lengths!" The announcer stated as the last of the horses crossed the wire.

Michael was looking over at her, but she wasn't sure how long he had been staring. Her face certainly reflected her thoughts, no doubt.

"Having fun?" he teased.

"At a horse-related event? Is that even a question?" she replied, lightly punching his arm.

For a moment, the old Emma and Michael had emerged.

With any luck, what happened between them could finally be swept under the rug, allowing who they used to be as friends to come back to the surface.

Maybe their earlier conversation had cleared the air once and for all?

There was no friend she wanted in her life more than Michael, that much had become clear to her during their hiatus. They walked back towards the truck, laughing as they talked.

Yes, she was glad things were getting back to how they once were.

Emma sat tall in the saddle, leaning back slightly on her seat bones. Hearing the words of her dressage training sessions with Ben ringing in her ears, she reminded herself that this was dressage and not the hunter ring, a habit that was proving hard to break. Using her seat to ask Nettie to slow her pace before asking with her rein aids, the mare broke back to a working trot underneath her. Making a twenty meter circle, she focused on the mare's bend and her own position.

Turning back towards the center line, she halted at X, managing to get the mare almost square as she stopped.

"What a good girl, Nettie!" Emma exclaimed, patting the horse's neck as she allowed her to walk off on a loose rein. It had been surprising at first how much she needed to use her body in dressage, especially in comparison to her years of hunters. Certainly it was a learning curve, but one she felt she was starting to come out of.

Heading out of the dressage ring, she headed out into the back field, towards the galloping path. Today was conditioning day, and it was a personal favorite of hers.

Emma asked Nettie for the canter, starting off at a medium pace, letting her stretch and settle into a steady rhythm. Feeling the rush of the impending forward pace, she sat up in the saddle, asking the horse to open up her stride into a hand gallop.

Hooves pounded on the path; wind whirled past her ears as the mare's nostrils flared with each footfall. To her, this was better than flying. Emma was enjoying getting to know Nettie and felt a strong bond with the mare already. It was exciting to think about competing a horse with so much experience, and she felt fortunate to be making her debut in eventing with a mount who knew what she was doing.

Walking back to the barns after a long gallop and cool down, she let her mind drift to her impending trip to Wellington. Seeing Liam after so much time had passed brought a mix of emotions. In a way, she sometimes felt like she was single since he was so far away. Of course, she spoke to him often, but that was hardly a replacement for being together in person.

Emma remembered how easy the relationship between them had been when they were both living in Wellington. But now, it felt like they lived two separate lives. Her mind began to drift to a memory of her and Liam when they first started dating, before all the mess with her stalker had starting interfering with her life...

"I'm getting in the ocean," Emma had said in a way that made it clear there was no talking her out of it.

"At night? Em, its pitch black out," Liam had said, tossing her a look that said she might be crazy if she did.

Emma had stared back out at the deep blue, almost black water, longingly. They had all but shut the restaurant down where they had dinner that night, and the bottle of wine they split had her feeling even more spirited than usual. Although, it never took much convincing to get Emma to the beach under any circumstances. In fact, this little night trip to the ocean had been her idea. They sat close, holding hands on the wooden lifeguard tower steps, certainly what Liam had envisioned when she had brought up the idea. But based on the look in his eye now, he hadn't expected her to actually get in the water.

"You know there are sharks in there, right? You won't be able to see them even if they are only a few feet away...," Liam began.

"I know, Liam," Emma said, cutting him off as she stood to her feet. "Don't worry, I'm only going in less than knee deep. Are you coming?"

Liam stared at the determined look on her face, his jaw open slightly, still unsure how else he could deter her. That was the problem though, and it seemed he was drawing that conclusion the longer she stood there, hands on her hips.

Emma turned towards the ocean with a devious smile and kicked off her sandals before running full speed toward the crashing waves. Her lightweight sundress flattened against her figure as she ran, flowing out behind her as it caught the wind coming off the water.

For Emma, there had always been this magnetic pull toward the ocean; it was so vast, so beautiful, at night especially, it felt incredibly powerful. She hadn't stopped running until her feet hit the foamy waves, and she stood there ankle deep as the wind whipped her hair around her.

It was hard to hear anything but the waves and wind, so she was pleasantly surprised when she felt Liam's arms wrapping around her waist, his head resting on her shoulder as he followed her gaze out to the horizon. The moon was so bright that night that their figures casted a shadow on the beach below them and made the water glitter slightly in the dim light. She remembered standing there like that with him for a long while, just staring out at the sea as the tide rolled in and out across her legs. At one point, Liam had released her from his embrace, stepped a few feet away and lightly kicked water in her direction. Turning his way, she stood, mouth agape, laughing as she chased the now running Liam down the beach, tackling him into another embrace when she finally reached him.

Their laughter echoed in her mind as she was pulled to the present, approaching the barns now.

"Can we ever be that couple again?" she thought, a bittersweet feeling still lingering in her mind after the memory.

New relationships are nothing like those that are well-established, especially when you're an adult. Emma wasn't naïve;

she knew that the puppy love stage didn't last forever. But she couldn't help but feel hers and Liam's was cut short but the incident with Bo stalking her and then living in different cities. Of course, she had signed up for this. It was something she had turmoiled over for weeks when she thought about where she would be taking a permanent job, knowing it would put strain on the relationship if she chose to live in Ocala. Did she regret her decision to stay here? Not once. Emma knew this is where she belonged, and each passing day solidified that. She could only hope she and Liam could find their footing being over three hours away and make it work. What choice did they have?

Some of the farm hands were in front of barn one as she approached, finishing up the morning's barn chores. Emma started riding early this morning to beat the heat and was glad she did so now that the temperature was rising.

"Good morning, Miss Emma," Hank said, and Don offered a warm smile and tip of his hat before picking up the wheelbarrow and heading toward the manure pile. Hank and Don had become a few of her favorites of Ben David's staff, along with Lily and Julia, of course. And rightly so; the two older gentlemen had worked for Ben David for over a decade now. She found them to be like two quirky uncles she never knew she needed, and they reminded her a little of the friendship she had formed with Mateo at Twin Oaks.

"Good morning, Hank, you too Don," Emma said, first turning to Hank who stood in front of her ready to take Nettie, and then Don who was halfway to his destination now. While she knew the workers here were willing to untack and cold hose any of Ben's horses she worked, she hardly took them up on that offer. Her years of never having that luxury at Maggie's and her time as a working student had hardwired that into her.

Even when she would be running Cathy's future farm, she couldn't imagine having horses tacked up or untacked for her. On the days she was busier and had extra work or horses to ride for Ben, she did hand a horse off to Don or Hank to be put away for her. Still, it was something she hated doing even when it was all but necessary when trying to get horses ridden before the heat of the day.

Today, unfortunately, was going to be one of those days. Emma had to work several horses that were normally ridden on Fridays, but since she was going to be in Wellington tomorrow, she was working them today instead. Not only was she working against the ever-rising temperature, but she still had to get back to her apartment at a reasonable hour to pack and hopefully get a good night's sleep since she planned to leave early in the morning.

Stepping into the shade of the barn, she smiled appreciatively to Hank as she handed Nettie's reins over to him. He led her down the barn aisle toward the wash bay, loosening her girth as they walked.

Walking toward the stall of the next horse she was exercising, Emma caught one of the farm hands, Clint, staring at her. She almost felt his gaze before she caught his expression. The way he stared at her was a look of utter disgust. His eyes had a venomous look about them, and the skin bunched between is eyes. At first, she wondered what she could have done to provoke such a reaction from him. Only seconds ago, she had handed Nettie over to Hank to be untacked and put away for her, so perhaps he felt some sort of discontent toward her for that?

That would make sense. After all, she had always felt a certain type of way towards those lucky few who could afford the luxury of having grooms to do the grunt work. Of course, she was not immune to the fact that for many professional riders with a long list of horses to ride, this was a necessity. Being at Three Phases Farm had made her realize that. However, she always felt it was impersonal and took away from the precious bonding time that happened between horse and rider as they prepared to ride or cared for them post-ride if it wasn't a necessity.

Clint was new to Three Phases Farm; she remembered that from Lily's introduction to the crew. He didn't know her and certainly couldn't know enough about her to understand that wasn't who she was as a horse person or a rider. For all the times she turned down the assistance from the farm hands before and after rides, was he really judging her so her harshly for this one day she asked for help?

From what she had overheard from the other staff, Clint was new to working with horses and to the area as well. She hoped in time he wouldn't look at her the way he was now. It made her sick to think anyone clumped her in the category of being too good to untack the horses she rode.

It crossed her mind to stop and say something to the young man burning holes into her with his eyes, but the moment she mustered the courage to do so, he dropped his gaze and went back to the manure he was picking from the stall.

It was probably for the best anyway; confronting him would only have caused awkwardness in the future.

Emma pulled a young bay gelding from his stall and led him to the grooming bay across from where Hank was now cold hosing Nettie. She fought the pang of guilt it brought to see him caring for her after the look Clint had just given her for doing so.

"You didn't really have a choice today," she reminded herself.

Focusing on the horse in front of her, she decided to let the anxiety of this situation go. The last thing she wanted was to carry this tension into her ride, especially on a young, green horse.

If she was lucky, maybe in the near future as she continued to work here, Clint would realize she was not the person he thought she was.

For now, she would just have to remind herself that she was not in fact, that person.

Chapter Four

Perhaps it was the fact that she was now a little over three hours south, but the sun seemed to shine just a little brighter in Wellington.

Or maybe it was just the excitement of seeing two people who were very important to her for the first time in a long time. More than likely it was the latter of the two, but what did she care?

Today was going to be a good day.

The sign in front of her officially welcomed her to the city limits of Wellington, and a flutter of anticipation bubbled up inside her. Her GPS said she was a mere ten minutes from Cathy and Liam's estate.

Palm trees lined almost every street she turned on, and looking at the scenery blurring past her, she almost felt like she had never left. It was also a bit of déjà vu of the first time she had arrived in this tropical pony paradise. While she was glad she lived in the rolling country hills of Ocala, she had to admit

Wellington was still one of her top favorite places to visit in Florida. And why wouldn't it be? It held so many of her favorite things. She had wondered if being back here would also bring back bitter memories of when Bo had stalked her, but she was pleasantly surprised that driving down these Wellington streets had not brought on any kind of PTSD.

Pulling into Cathy's long driveway, she put her car in park as quickly as she could before throwing open her car door.

Liam was already walking through the now open front door of the estate and met her halfway down the walkway as she all but leapt into his arms. Kissing sweetly, she released him long enough to look him in the eye before wrapping her arms around his neck once more.

"I missed you," she whispered, still hanging onto him an extra moment before releasing him from her grasp.

"I missed you too," Liam said, both hands still wrapped around her.

"There's our girl!" Emma heard Aunt Cathy's voice say behind Liam. Emma took two quick steps, closing the gap between her and Cathy as she launched herself into the woman's warm embrace.

"My dear, we have missed you!" Cathy said, looking Emma up and down. "We need to get this tiny thing something to eat though," Cathy added, looping her arm through Emma's as she led her towards the front door.

"I ride a lot of horses," Emma said, smiling and giving Cathy a half shrug as her excuse.

"I suppose we will just have to fatten you up while you're here now, won't we?" Cathy replied.

Oh how she had missed sweet, eccentric Aunt Cathy. She felt almost like a second mother to her now, her "Florida mom" as she had sometimes affectionately called her.

Cathy led Emma through the familiar estate, with Liam trailing close behind, towards the back door leading to the courtyard. It was just as stunning as she remembered. Of course, Cathy had gone all out and had a table covered in several types of lunch type food and sandwiches that was clearly set up by a caterer. Several bottles of champagne were sitting in a galvanized ice bucket on a table next to the food.

"Cathy you shouldn't have...," Emma began, knowing by now that it was no use.

"Well of course I did dear, it's been far too long since you were here," Cathy added quickly.

Emma supposed there was no use letting good food go to waste, and she hadn't eaten since breakfast before she left Ocala, so she headed straight for the table of food.

Liam popped open the first bottle of champagne, pouring it into three champagne flutes. Her mouth watered looking at the bubbly champagne in the glass he handed her, knowing Cathy only bought the good stuff.

"Cheers," Liam said, raising his glass to eye level.

"Cheers," Cathy and Emma said almost in unison, glasses clinking together.

It felt so good to get away from daily life, and Emma always felt like she was on some fancy tropical getaway when she was at this estate. They sat at the table, shaded by an umbrella, across from the pool and began catching up.

"Liam, how has your job been going?" Emma asked him. They hadn't talked much about his work over the phone lately, mostly because by the time they were both done with their respectively long days it just wasn't something he seemed interested in discussing. She supposed if she was doing anything short of what she was passionate about, that she would probably feel the same way. But she figured in person, with a glass of champagne in their hands, it was a lighter topic of conversation.

"Good, but busy as you know. I'm still running to job sites both locally and out of town three times a week. It's been a lot to learn, but I think I'm starting to feel comfortable in my position," Liam replied.

"Of course you are dear, it's in your blood. Your father was exceptional at his work," Cathy said, putting her hand over Liam's.

"I just hope I can live up to his legacy," Liam said, a slight sadness in his eyes. Emma realized this might be the first time he had truly spoken about his father other than when he told her back at college when he mentioned his father's passing and then once more when he told her about his parents passing away when he was a child. She had always wondered about them, and how often Liam thought about them all these years later. Emma had also always wondered if Liam's Aunt Cathy was his father or mother's sister.

"May I ask, was Liam's father your brother?" she asked softly. The way Cathy looked at Liam as she spoke, she had a hunch that he was.

"Yes. His name was Benjamin. He was a wonderful father and brother. I think about him almost every day still," she said, tossing a bereaved look towards Liam who met her gaze with a similar sadness. Dabbing the corner of her eyes with a handkerchief she pulled from her pocket, she waved her hand in the air dismissively.

"Alright, enough of the heavy talk," Cathy stated.

"I'm sorry...," Emma began, but Cathy cut her off.

"Nonsense, talking about someone who has passed keeps them alive through us. Now, Emma, why don't you tell us all about how training is going at Ben David's barn?" Cathy asked.

Emma was happy to ramble on about all the horses she was working with, how Valentine was doing, and her training with Ben David.

"That's wonderful dear, I'm glad you're settling in there. I do have some good news on that front, actually. I have finally worked everything out with my accountant and financial advisors so we have the finances ready to go once we find the right property. I will probably head up there for a few days in a couple weeks so we can start looking at properties," Cathy said.

"Cathy, that's great news! I can't tell you how excited I am and honored that you want me helping you run the place," Emma replied.

"Not helping, honey, you *will* be running the place," Cathy said.

A shiver of nerves and excitement ran through her body at the thought. Every other day she felt like she switched from feeling ready to take on such an incredible responsibility to not feeling ready at all; it just depended on the day. But this was it, the homestretch of a reality she couldn't have even dreamed about not so long ago.

Less than a year ago her whole life was crumbling around her, heartbroken from her last relationship and her future in jeopardy. Now, here she sat with her boyfriend and his aunt talking about the farm she would be running.

It certainly was funny what time could do.

"Emma, come with me a moment. I have a surprise for you," Cathy said, standing up.

Emma shot a quizzical look at Liam, who offered a clueless shrug about what Cathy had in store for her. Although, she wasn't all that surprised; she wouldn't put it past Cathy to keep something from Liam knowing he would spill the beans.

Emma followed behind Cathy as she led the way back into the house and up the grand, winding staircase. Their home had six bedrooms, and Cathy stopped at the last one on the left, the room she typically stayed in when she stayed the night.

"Close your eyes," Cathy prompted, turning around to make sure Emma actually had them shut. She heard a door open and the sound of plastic moving but Emma kept them sealed, knowing there would be hell to pay if Cathy caught her peeking.

"Ok, you can open them now," Cathy said about thirty seconds later.

Emma's eyes flew open and locked onto a black high-low style dress that looked entirely too expensive. The top part cut into a deep v neck with a thin piece of nude mesh across it, and it was covered in tiny glittering beads that ran to just where her waist met her hips. The bottom was silky and the highest part hit just above the knee while the back had a slight train.

Emma caught her breath as she studied the details of the dress.

"Cathy, this dress is...well, it's stunning," she stammered, reaching out her fingers to touch the silky fabric.

"It's for the charity gala tomorrow. I know you said you had a formal dress already, but I went dress shopping and couldn't help myself," Cathy said, draping the dress across Emma's body and turning her to face the full-length mirror across the room.

Sure, Emma had a used prom dress she found at a local re-sale shop for thirty dollars. This, however, was by far the most beautiful dress she had ever seen, let alone worn. Unexpected tears welled in her eyes; she could blame the champagne, but really it was the kindness Cathy had shown by purchasing such an elaborate dress for her that had brought her to tears.

"Cathy I...thank you," she managed to get out before her voice broke. For once, Cathy said nothing but pulled Emma into her arms. She gathered Emma's hair, laying it to one side of her neck, studying the way it looked against the dress. Setting the dress down on the bed, Cathy took Emma's hand, meeting her gaze.

"I couldn't have children of my own. It's not something I like talking about, but I have Liam, so my heart has always been full because of it. But deep down, I think part of me still wished I could have had a daughter of my own. Dear, you are like the daughter I never had, so you're just going to have to let me spoil you a little, ok?" Cathy said, her own smile cracking a little with emotion.

Emma smiled back, lip quivering. There were no words for how much she loved and appreciated Cathy, and she would probably never feel quite deserving of everything she had already done for her.

"Don't show Liam the dress. Let's keep it a surprise for tomorrow, shall we?" Cathy said with a wink.

"Deal," Emma replied, dabbing tears from her own eyes now.

They walked back down the winding staircase and were back to talking and laughing by the time they reached the table where Liam still sat. His eyes flitted from Emma to Cathy, and his face wore a curious expression.

"So, is anyone going to tell me what the surprise was?" Liam asked, although his voice already had a hint of defeat.

"Of course not, you will just have to wait until tomorrow," Cathy said, touching his shoulder lightly before sitting back down.

"I had a feeling that's what you would say," Liam said taking a sip of his champagne and shaking his head.

"Sorry," Emma said, shooting him an apologetic look. She was sure Liam knew she had been sworn to secrecy as well.

"I'll go get another bottle of champagne," Liam said, his hand catching Emma's as he headed towards the table. She watched him walk away, then glanced back at Cathy whose content smile lingered.

For a moment, Emma pretended that she never had to leave.

Emma heard a knock on her guest bedroom door at Cathy's estate. Opening it a crack, she saw Cathy standing in the doorway dressed in a floor length maroon dress covered in sequins.

"My, Emma, you look radiant," Cathy said as Emma opened the door the rest of the way.

"Thank you, and so do you! Do you mind?" Emma said, turning to show Cathy the back of the dress that she had only managed to zip up halfway.

"It would be my pleasure," Cathy said, gently tugging the zipper the rest of the way.

Turning around to face the mirror, Emma smoothed the dress as she admired its beauty.

"This dress is truly stunning Cathy, thank you again."

"Liam is going to lose his mind when he sees you in it," Cathy said, placing her hands on either side of Emma's shoulders, looking in the mirror as she threw her a wink.

Emma grabbed the clutch purse she had packed with a few essentials and followed Cathy into the hallway. Pausing to gather her dress, she began walking down the stairs.

Liam's eyes widened when she came into view and quickly offered her his hand to help her down the remaining stairs.

"Emma, you look incredible," he said, kissing her on the cheek.

"You clean up pretty well yourself," she teased, admiring him in his black tuxedo. This was the first time she had seen him dress in formal clothing, and she had to admit, she felt a little like they were headed to prom.

"Alright you two, the car is waiting for us outside!" Cathy said, all but shooing them towards the front door.

Twenty minutes later, the car pulled into the parking lot of the venue where the gala was being held. Emma was both excited and surprised to see that it was directly off the A1A, which is the road running parallel to the ocean.

Liam took her hand, helping her and his Aunt Cathy from the vehicle and they headed up the short flight of stairs that led to the entrance. Walking into the massive ballroom style venue, Emma felt her jaw dropping a little but slammed it shut before anyone saw. A crystal chandelier hung in the center of the wood dance floor, and what had to be almost a hundred tables surrounded it. A table on one side of the room had a silent auction, and an impressive looking bar was on the other side. People in black tie attire mingled at tables or clustered together in different parts of the room. Waiters and waitresses in uniform scurried around, preparing tables and passing out glasses of champagne.

"Shall we find our table?" Cathy asked, interrupting Emma's gawking. Nodding, Emma, and Cathy looped an arm through Liam's on either side of him as they headed to the table.

The charity's host welcomed the attendees a little while later, announcing that the six-course meal would be served momentarily. Emma tried to hide her surprise; she wasn't even sure she knew that many courses existed and she definitely didn't know what could possibly be served for the courses before the main course and dessert.

It was like a mini surprise every time the waiter showed up with yet another mini meal. By the time they were served all six courses, which consisted of hors d'oeuvres, soup, appetizer, salad, main course, and dessert, it felt as if they had been seated and eating for two hours.

The live band started up not long after the final course was served, and she resisted the urge to slump in her chair. How are people who eat six courses expected to dance?

By the fourth song the band played, she couldn't take sitting there any longer.

"Dance with me?" Emma asked as she stood from her chair, reaching her hand out to Liam.

"Why, of course, Miss Walker," Liam said in a playful tone. Emma was surprised at how well Liam could dance, although, she suspected that being raised by Cathy had something to do with that.

He spun her around before dipping her, catching her at the perfect time and launching her back on her feet with ease.

"Liam Anderson, you never told me you could dance like that," Emma said, grinning at him face to face as the song ended.

"Aunt Cathy," was all he said, confirming her suspicion.

The band started up again, playing a slow song that brought new couples to the dance floor. Liam wrapped one hand around her back and took her left hand in his as they fell into the rhythm of the sweet slow love song playing in the background.

"I've missed this. Us, I mean," Emma said. It had been hard being so far from Liam these last couple of months. Being together the last two days, however, felt like they had never been apart. She wished their relationship could be this simple all the time.

"I have too," he murmured pulling her closer. They swayed back and forth to the beat of the music and Emma rested her head on his shoulder.

"May I cut in?" Aunt Cathy asked as she approached after the song had ended, leaving Emma and Liam standing still, still holding one another's gaze.

"Of course," Emma said, as she headed to the edge of the dance floor.

The band picked up with a mid-tempo song, and Emma watched as Liam spun his aunt around the dance floor. She smiled, watching Cathy beam and Liam laugh as they glided across the floor. If she hadn't known them, she would have assumed Cathy was Liam's mother and not his aunt. Although, she knew Cathy loved Liam like her own and she was sure Liam felt the same about his aunt.

Her own mother had always told her to watch how a man treats his mother; it's a surefire way to see how he will treat you once the honeymoon phase wears off. Watching Liam and Cathy now, she couldn't help considering her mother's wisdom.

She figured now would be a good time to step outside and get some air and let Liam spend another song or so with his aunt. She headed towards where she had seen other guests coming in and out of a set of glass doors on the backside of the venue.

Pushing them open, she was hit with a gust of salty air. Grinning, she stepped further out onto the lengthy patio that hovered over the sandy beach below. Emma could hear waves crashing in the distance, although it was too dark out to see them. Hanging over the railing at the edge of the patio, she closed her eyes letting the ocean wind blow across her face.

"Em, you ok?" Liam's concerned voice asked behind her a few minutes later.

"Liam, you didn't have to follow me out here. I was just taking in the view while you danced with your aunt," Emma said, briefly looking behind her before setting her gaze back on the invisible waves in the distance.

"Don't worry, Aunt Cathy was already complaining about her feet being tired anyway. She sent me out here," Liam replied.

That, she believed.

Liam wrapped his arms around her, resting his chin on her shoulder as he followed her gaze to the dark horizon. They spent a few moments in silence, listening to the chatter of guests at the other end of the patio and the waves crashing rhythmically in front of them.

"I was just thinking the other day about that night on the beach when we first started dating. Do you remember it?"

"You mean the one where you insisted on getting in the water in the middle of the night? Oh, I remember," he said, chuckling.

"Standing out here, I was just thinking about it again," Emma said wistfully. Emma turned to face Liam, locking her eyes into his. Her eyes held a sadness in them.

"What's wrong, Em?" he prodded, sensing she was holding back.

"Can we take a walk?" she replied, glancing around at the crowd that began to gather on the patio now that the band was taking a break.

Saying nothing, he took her hand and helped her down the set of stairs that led from the patio to the beach.

Gathering her dress in one hand, they strolled a little way from the venue towards a group of large rocks that lined the beach. Sitting on one, she let out a sigh. This was a conversation she didn't want to have but at this point, she couldn't avoid it anymore.

"Liam, this long-distance thing…," Emma trailed off, shifting on the rock uncomfortably.

"I just don't know how we are going to make this work long term. You're so busy with your job, I'm busy with mine, and we hardly see each other. We talk, but it doesn't feel like it's enough sometimes. Being here with you this weekend, it made me realize how much I missed this, being *with* you. In person, I don't have any doubts about us. But back home...," she cut herself off by standing up, not able to sit still another second longer while her words came pouring out.

Liam pulled her in, kissing her before she had a chance to say anything else. Pulling away, he placed both hands on either side of her face.

"Emma Walker, I love you. I've never met anyone I felt this way about until I met you. I know a long-distance relationship is hard, but we can figure it out," Liam stated, his eyes reflecting his feelings perfectly.

Blinking in shock, she stared back into his light blue eyes, searching them for answers. He had never told her he loved her before, and she had not expected him to say it tonight. Certainly not after she had all but told him long distance was taking a toll on their relationship.

Liam was still locked into her gaze, waiting for her to say something.

Anything.

Was she in love with Liam? She had considered saying those three little words to him so many times. But she had always stopped herself for several reasons. One, she wanted to be sure. Two, she had no interest in scaring him off if she said it too soon.

So, was she ready to say it now? Being here in Wellington the last few days with Liam certainly had confirmed her feelings for him. But that still changed nothing about their situation; they lived more than three hours apart.

"Liam, I care about you so much and when we are together, I feel like everything is right in my world. But...," she looked away from him a moment, hoping his good looks and intent stare might help her think clearly enough to form the words she needed.

"I don't know that I can say those words to you until we figure out where things are headed between us," Emma continued.

"Emma, I love you, and I see a future with you. What more do you need?" Liam asked, hurt in his voice now.

Emma pulled away from his touch, her forehead scrunching. Biting her lip, she tried not to let her emotions overwhelm her.

"What are we supposed to do Liam, see each other once every few weeks and talk on the phone once a day for twenty minutes about nothing in particular? How can we possibly have a future like that?" Emma replied, her voice shaking a little with emotion.

"We can figure it out...," Liam began.

"How?!" Emma asked. Turning around, she took three steps toward the dark waves, closed her eyes and clenched her fists. Taking a few deep breaths, she turned back around.

"I'm sorry, I didn't mean to get so upset. I just...well I just don't see how things can be simply figured out," she said, taking his hand again. He didn't seem to have an answer for her, and stared back at her with a pained expression.

"We don't have to figure this out tonight," Liam finally replied quietly.

"You're right. Let's go back and try to enjoy the rest of the night, ok?" Emma said, softer this time.

Liam took her hand again as they headed down the beach back toward the venue. She glanced his way now and then, catching his sad, thoughtful expression. Perhaps he was considering her words? She felt a pang of guilt that she hadn't told him she loved him too. He had to be feeling a little bit hurt by that. It had almost escaped her lips more than once as they walked, but she felt it wasn't the right time given how the conversation had unfolded and her doubts about how they were going to make their situation work long term.

Forcing a smile back on her face for Cathy's sake, they headed back into the ballroom.

Excusing herself without giving a reason why, she headed to the bar across the room to get a drink. Liam certainly would have offered or insisted on getting it for her had he known. But right now, she wanted a minute to herself.

By the time she was back at the table, she had decided to lock up her doubts about their future for the rest of the night so she could enjoy what was left of it.

Liam pulled her back on the dance floor as another slow song started up.

Laying her head on his shoulder, she closed her eyes and soaked up the scent of his cologne and the little things about this moment.

This would be a moment she would need to go back to in her mind during the next long stretch of not seeing him, and she knew it.

Chapter Five

This evening, she was glad to be going on a nonchalant hack with Lily.

It had been a long and busy first day back at Three Phases Farm after returning home from her trip to Wellington yesterday.

Leading Valentine from the barn and into the now cooler evening air, she saw Lily swinging a leg over her horse, Annie, as she stepped a few feet away waiting for Emma. Mounting up, she nudged her mare forward, walking parallel with Lily's mare.

"I can't believe this is only the second time we've done this," Lily said, shifting as she settled into her saddle.

"I know, we should make it a weekly thing," Emma replied, taking in the scenery around her.

The young women headed toward the empty galloping path, ready to make a complete circle around the property should daylight allow them to do so.

"So, tell me everything about your Wellington trip," Lily asked, glancing Emma's way and smiling.

"What happened?" Lily added, looking concerned now as she read her friend's expression. Emma's face clearly gave away that things hadn't been all rainbows and butterflies during the trip.

Emma relayed the events of her night on the beach with Liam.

"Oh Em, I'm sorry your trip didn't go as planned. I know you were looking forward to seeing Liam after being apart so long. How were things between you two yesterday before you left?" Lily asked.

"All right, I guess. Maybe a little bit awkward, but I can tell his feelings for me still haven't changed. We didn't talk about the real problem of being long distance after our discussion on the beach though, and I doubt we will until we are in person again. He told me he loved me again as we were saying goodbye, and I just stood there trying to think of what to say back. Of course, I reminded him how much I care about him, which I do. But the fact that things are still the way they are is keeping me from saying it back, you know?" Emma said, shaking her head as she recalled the emotions of the weekend.

"I get it. Remember my college boyfriend, Chris? One month into my internship here, and we just fell apart. It was for the best though, and honestly, I'm glad it ended sooner than later so it wasn't constantly distracting me to think about someone so far away. Sorry, I know that probably doesn't make you feel any better about your situation," Lily said as she shot Emma a sympathetic look.

"No, I think you're right. Long distance relationships are just too hard, and that's why I'm so conflicted. I wanted so badly to just ask him right out if he ever had any intentions of moving here, but I was afraid if I did, I would get an answer I didn't like. If he isn't even open to moving ever, where does that leave us?" Emma asked.

"Well, I hope you know I'm here if you ever need to talk," Lily said.

"Thanks Lil, I appreciate that. I'm glad I have you here to talk to. I think I would have packed up and moved home by now if it weren't for you living here as well," Emma replied.

"Of course, and trust me, I feel the same way. Us horse girls got to stick together, right?" Lily tossed another sympathetic look at her friend. "Let's change the subject and get your mind off Liam for a while. Speaking of friendships though, it seems you and Michael are still doing well, as friends I mean. I'm sure it's harder since you don't work together every day, but you seemed to have fun at the racetrack, right?" Lily asked.

Emma sighed audibly. It wasn't Lily's fault that most of the relationships in her life seemed to be entirely too complicated right now.

"Lily, I consider you one of my best friends now. I know we were not nearly as close back home, but let's face it, moving here changed everything for us both," Emma said, pausing after she spoke, unsure if she was ready to spill the secret she had held onto for so long now.

Lily tossed Emma a quizzical look and they continued down the galloping path at a leisurely walk, their horses' ears were pricked forward, unaware of the intense conversation between their owners.

"Of course, and I'm so glad we are closer now, but where is this coming from?" Lily asked curiously.

"There's something I've been keeping from you and from every-one, even Mandy when we have our weekly talks on the phone. But I think it's time for me to get this off my chest and tell someone, and I want you to be the one I confide in. So, can you promise what I am about to tell you stays between us?" Emma asked.

"Em, of course. I hope you know you can tell me anything," Lily replied.

Emma looked out at the horizon, blowing out her breath slowly, preparing her words before she spoke to them.

"The night of the Million Dollar Grand Prix party at Twin Oaks, Michael walked me to my guesthouse and he kissed me," Emma said, her words tumbling out.

"He what?!" Lily said, her eyes wide.

"To be fair, he and, well, all of us had been drinking quite a bit that night. Not that it's an excuse for his impulsive behavior, but I doubt he would have done what he did sober. Anyway, he apologized immediately and told me to forget it ever happened, but things were definitely awkward between us for a while, and still kind of are. We talked about the kiss at the racetrack for the first time, but I didn't have the nerve to ask him why he did it. If he did or does have feelings for me and admitted it, that would change everything between us. More so than the kiss even did," Emma said.

"Does Liam know?" Lily asked, a look of shock still on her face.

"No, and if I can avoid it, he never will. What's the point, you know? It will only hurt him or make him hate Michael, and I just can't lose Michael's friendship. Not to mention my relationship with Liam is hard enough right now...him knowing about this would only strain things between us more. Or ruin them entirely," Emma said.

Saying out loud all the emotions she had been dealing with made it sound worse than it had in her head. When did things get so complicated?

"I don't even know what to say, Em. That's a lot to keep bottled up all this time. I'm glad you told me, and please don't worry, your secret is safe with me," Lily assured her.

Emma smiled somberly at her friend, thankful she had her in her life, especially for moments like this.

Their horses plodded along lazily as they rounded the turn that looped them back toward the barn. Emma was glad Lily had fallen silent, not pressing for any further details.

Trapped in her own mind now, Emma mulled over what the future of her relationship with Liam and her friendship with Michael might look like.

The first of morning's light peeked around the live oaks scattered in the pastures of Three Phases Farm. Unlatching the gate that led to the pasture Valentine was in, Emma stepped off the gravel and onto the dewy grass as she headed in the direction of her mare, whose gaze had already locked onto her owner.

The pre-horse show jitters were already buzzing around her brain as she thought about the day's events. It was her and Valentine's first eventing trial, but she was thankful that she would at least be riding the experienced Nettie in a few phases before it was time to compete Valentine. She had also promised to take one of the younger, green off-the-track Thoroughbreds Ben David had as a sale project so he could get some more milage. Luckily, this was the gelding's third competition, and it was only slightly unsettling that this youngster had more eventing experience than she did.

"You got this," she told herself, only half believing her own mind's pep talk.

Valentine walked the few remaining steps towards Emma, ears pricked as her owner ran her hand up the mare's face, playing with her forelock.

"You ready to gallop and jump some stuff today, lady?" she murmured to the mare. Even if her horse could talk, she already knew what her answer would be. Of course she was game to gallop around cross country or tear up the stadium ring. What she was still a little concerned about, however, was the dressage phase. Valentine had made progress in her training, but her mare still considered dressage a very boring and lengthy warm-up that could be better spent jumping around.

Slipping the horse's head through her halter, Emma led her to the gate and out of the pasture, still turning over the possible outcomes of the day.

Lily smiled from the grooming bay across from where Emma was now cross-tying her horse.

"Any regrets on turning her out the day before a show?" Lily asked, looking Valentine up and down for grass or manure stains.

"Are you kidding? I would rather deal with her being covered in mud this morning than the consequences of not turning her out the night before a competition," Emma replied.

Emma knew her mare inside and out at this point. She had learned the hard way that keeping her horse inside the night before to save her a little sleep and grooming time was not worth the repercussions. Valentine was the type of horse who needed her outside time. This mare was a different beast when she was turned out versus kept inside, and it was especially not worth the extra spunk she would have encountered today had she kept her inside. She wasn't the slightest bit worried about her horse 'not having enough gas in the tank' so to speak; this girl had endless batteries.

Turning on the hose, she began spraying the white socks on the mare's legs which had, as she expected, turned a brownish green color.

"Still worth it," she thought, pulling out the purple shampoo that always transformed even the dirtiest white legs back to a snow-white color.

Allowing her mare's legs and other spots she had touched up with a sponge to dry, she pulled Nettie out of her stall. Fortunately, Nettie was not the type of horse that absolutely had to be turned out the night before. Emma could only imagine how much time her flea-bitten grey coat would have taken to perfect. Brushing her with a soft brush before addressing the minimal spots she had managed to get dirty overnight, she took this time to connect with the mare on the ground. She took the mare's head in her hands and met her gaze, scratching her favorite spots behind her ears. It was something Maggie had taught her from an early age, and it stuck with her even all these years later.

After she wrapped up with Nettie, Emma pulled Lenny out, the young off-the-track Thoroughbred she was also riding today and was relieved to see his dark bay coat had managed to stay almost completely clean.

"Len, you are the only one who I don't have to groom for an hour today," Emma said with a laugh as she took some time to connect with the gelding as well.

Emma heard the truck and empty trailer rattling in the distance, growing louder as it approached. Lily and Emma exchanged glances, hearing it at the same time.

"Want to start getting horses ready to load?" Lily asked, saying what Emma was already thinking.

"Yep. Let's do this," she said, unclipping Lenny from the cross ties.

Hank hopped out of the truck and dropped the ramp down before heading towards the pile of show tack trunks and tack that they had already stacked up earlier that morning.

When the last horse was loaded in the trailer, Emma and Lily, along with Don, who also acted as a groom at times, hopped into the truck. Lily had already informed Emma that Ben usually drove separately and would be meeting them at the show grounds.

The show grounds were not terribly far from their farm, and Emma rolled her window down to get a good look at the grounds as they pulled into the entrance. The cross country field came into view on her right, and she felt a wave of excitement at the course that wound in and out of live oaks with the occasional palm tree scattered around.

Hank parked the truck and trailer near the row of temporary stalls they had reserved, and they got to work unloading the horses and tack.

It wasn't until they were checking in at the show office that her nerves found her again. She found it odd that even after showing so many times over the years that she still got butterflies. Emma was sure that some of it had to do with the fact that despite her research and what Ben David had told her, competing in an eventing trial was still an unknown.

But as she tacked Nettie, she felt a sense of relief that the experienced mare would have her back as she navigated her way through the unfamiliar phases.

They headed to the dressage warm-up ring where Ben David sat in a folding chair next to his barn manager, Julia, deep in conversation.

"Ah, there she is! How are you feeling today?" Ben asked Emma.

"A little nervous, but prepared," Emma said, hoping she didn't sound like a scared teenager at her first horse how. Although, she had to admit, she was getting a lot of first-time horse show vibes from this day already.

"Good. Let's go ahead and warm up Nettie and remember the things we worked on with her. Less is more with your reins and lots of rhythm control with your seat," Ben instructed.

Emma nodded as she walked Nettie into the warm-up ring. As much as she adored Valentine, she couldn't help but enjoy how easy and well-schooled Nettie was. She hoped with the same milage her own horse would feel this fancy.

Untacking Nettie after what felt like three fairly successful phases with her, Emma felt ready to get back out there with young Lenny. Nettie had obediently performed her dressage test, (more importantly, Emma had not forgotten her dressage pattern despite her fear of doing so), and they had gone clear in stadium jumping and cross country.

Don took Nettie from her after she gave the mare a well-deserved pat and a horse cookie. Her round with Lenny felt uneventful, although she did take a rail down in stadium and had a small time fault in cross country. Now, it was time to focus on her own horse.

Valentine eyed her owner curiously as she approached her stall with her tack. Emma swore this mare understood why she was here, and she seemed eager to get out on course every time.

The now tacked up Valentine power walked with Emma aboard toward the dressage warm-up ring. Her ears were hyper focused on the activity in front of her. Walking her into the warm-up ring,

Emma focused on her position first, then Valentine's bend, and her contact in the reins. She reminded herself to relax as she did every competition. Her mare fed so easily off her emotions, and it certainly did not take much to turn her into a ball of tension, which was less than ideal for dressage.

Gingerly asking for the trot, Valentine offered a quicker pace than Emma had hoped for, forcing her to post slowly as she circled in hopes this would help slow her mare's roll. After a few laps around the ring, she felt the mare start to relax through her back, flicking an ear back toward Emma when she spoke to her. Her canter felt balanced and relaxed as well as they continued their warm-up, working through transitions multiple times.

"She looks good, Emma; how is she feeling?" Ben asked when they stopped where he was standing near the gate.

"More relaxed than she started out, but I think we are ready to go," Emma replied.

The stewardess nodded and signaled to them to enter the ring.

Emma took deep breaths, calming herself for her mare's sake as they entered the area that surrounded the dressage ring. She felt Valentine tense slightly as they walked around the little white dressage fence. To Emma's horror, she saw that from this angle the stadium jumping ring that sat at the top of a hill was much more visible here than it was in the warm-up ring. The mare's head flung up as she eyed the horse on course cantering by.

"Later Val," Emma whispered to the mare, hoping to convey that she just needed to make it through this phase in order to get to the fun stuff Valentine clearly wanted to do instead. The judge rang her bell signaling Emma could enter the ring.

Asking her horse for the trot, she attempted to focus the mare's attention off the other ring and back on her. The little chestnut seemed torn but managed to trot somewhat relaxed, albeit at a quicker pace than Emma would have preferred.

"I'll take what I can get at this point," she thought, posting as slowly as she could and trying to keep out of the mare's face, which would be asking for a fight.

They trotted down the center line at a pace she knew was still too fast for a working trot but kept her composure anyway as they headed into their first twenty-meter circle.

They headed down the long side, and Emma felt Valentine's body anticipate the dreaded canter transition.

"Relax!" she thought, sitting deep in the saddle as she asked for the canter. While she wouldn't call her canter transition explosive per se, it certainly wasn't calm; that was going to cost them a few points. They completed their twenty-meter circle and headed down the long side of the ring at the canter.

It was the next few moments that Emma would recall later as a bit of a blur.

Valentine's head flew up, her eyes locked onto something in the distance. The jumper ring again, perhaps? Before Emma had time to react, her mare grabbed the bit and began all but bolting towards the far side of the dressage ring.

It was the last two seconds before the mare's hooves left the ground that she realized she had actually locked on to the little white dressage ring fence. It was too late at that point though since they were already in the air, landing moments later.

Pulling her mare to a halt on the other side of the dressage ring, Emma felt her face flush red; she was mortified. The mare seemed offended by her owner's reaction. Certainly, Valentine thought she had simply cleared the first very tiny warm-up fence of the day.

Turning back toward the judge's booth, she heard one judge yell, "You can go back in and school!" A kind gesture for sure, and one she really had no choice but to take the judge up on. No way could she let this be how she ended her round. She needed to go back in and school for a few minutes for training purposes.

Of course, that didn't make the wide-eyed stares from the spectators, trainers, and other riders around her burn any less. Emma would have much rather continued cantering far, far away from the dressage ring where she could wallow in her wounded pride alone.

"But, that's not what equine professionals do," she reminded herself.

Pushing her own feelings aside, she asked the mare to trot on as she headed towards the entrance of the dressage arena again. Circling and asking for the canter like she had before things went terribly wrong, Emma kept the mare bent and focused on her aides as she headed out of the turn and back towards the long side of the ring. The mare picked up her pace, eyes flitting back toward the part of the ring she had just jumped, but Emma reminded her with the outside rein that wasn't what she wanted. Managing to stay in the ring the rest of the round, she saluted to the judge and thanked her for allowing her to go back into school before making her exit.

Ben, Julia, Lily, and Michael, who must have arrived just in time to see this ugly dressage round, stood at the edge of the arena where they had been watching with the same sympathetic looks on their faces.

"*I feel sick,*" she thought, slapping a smile on her face as she hid her internal turmoil.

"I don't know what happened. I know she was pretty distracted by the stadium jumping ring before we went in. As soon as we rounded the corner toward that ring at the canter it was like she went full throttle jumper mode," Emma said with a heavy sigh.

"It's her first time in a dressage ring off property. It can only get better from here, right?" Lily replied, shooting her a reassuring look.

"Right," Emma said, hoping Lily was right. At home, her horse had never attempted to jump out of the ring, but here, in her horse's mind, going to shows meant one thing: jumping.

The thing about eventing that Emma knew but hadn't truly considered until now, was that every phase's score counted. At the end of the day, this dressage score was going to come back to haunt her.

Back at the show stable, she switched out her tack and put on her safety vest as she prepared for the jumping rounds, trying to clear her mind of her less-than-ideal dressage round.

Valentine carelessly lipped at the hay in the corner of her show stall, oblivious that her actions had caused her owner the embarrassment it had. Emma pulled her horse's head up, resting her chin on the bridge of her mare's nose briefly before kissing her. Sliding the bridle over her ears, she promised herself not to hold the outburst against her horse as they headed to their next phase.

The jumping ring warm-up ring was busy, and riders called out jumps every few seconds as everyone vied for a chance to get a few fences under their belt before they headed into the arena for their turn. Valentine was on high alert now, jigging as they approached the entrance to the warm-up ring. Her body language seemed to say, "Oh, we are finally jumping? Now this I understand!"

Emma saw Michael wave from the far side of the warm-up ring. Emma gave a quick wave back before returning her focus back on her horse. It was nice he had showed up to support her, although, she hoped the rest of the day wouldn't be as embarrassing as it started out.

They cantered off, and her horse found her powerful on course canter with ease. She lapped the ring, changing direction and leads several times before Emma considered taking a jump. The ring was slightly less crowded now as a few of the riders were standing by the in-gate watching the current rider on course.

She pointed her mare towards the first warm-up jump, and Valentine charged it down with her usual enthusiasm, jumping it with room to spare. Emma couldn't help but smile; her mare's love for jumping was contagious. She looped around, taking the other fence set at their competition height, and found a deeper spot this time. Valentine jumped it round and clear, landing with a head shake.

With a pat, Emma ended Valentine's warming up there. She knew from experience it was best to take a couple fences and be done before Valentine got any spicier than she already was.

A couple rounds later and they were entering the stadium jumping arena themselves. Butterflies fluttered in her gut and her horse danced in place as they waited for the whistle to blow. Not to her surprise, her horse cantered off the moment they were signaled to start.

Emma remembered being pleasantly surprised at how nicely eventing stadium courses flowed. It was like a winding path versus the endless rollbacks and sharp turns of show jumping. Certainly, there were some tricky turns, but it felt almost easy in comparison to what she was used to.

Landing off fence number one, Emma reveled in her horse's power as she turned and took the next fence with ease. Setting her up, they took the first fence of a six-stride line, coming into a deep spot but clearing it with room to spare. Powering around a few of the individual fences, she pointed Valentine towards a dressed-up oxer which didn't seem to faze her in the least. Every competition with her horse reminded her of the same thing: this mare was born to be in the jumper ring.

Landing off the final jump, Emma felt a glimmer of hope as she patted her mare on the neck, letting her continue to roll out under her until they reached the gate.

"A clear round within the time for Emma Walker and Valentine," the announcer stated as they exited the ring. Lily, whose arms hung over the side of the fence where she had been watching, smiled and shook her head.

"She sure does love to jump, doesn't she?" Lily asked with a laugh.

"That she does," Emma said, patting her mare's glistening neck once more.

Feeling a twinge of hope that they wouldn't stay in the dead last position that the dressage phase had surely put them in, Emma headed towards the warm-up area for cross country. The grassy, open field sat parallel to the start box and had two logs as well as three tables of varied heights. Walking the perimeter of this warm-up area, she let her horse catch her breath as she recalled the cross country course in her mind.

She hoped if she could pull off a second clear round so they would at least land in a much less embarrassing placing for the day.

Cantering towards the first log after a walk break, Valentine charged eagerly at the natural jump, clearing it and hunting down the next. She felt good about how her horse was taking them out of stride as she landed off the table and brought her horse down to a walk.

"That's good enough," she said, scratching her horse under her mane as they walked towards the start box. Much like stadium jumping, there was no reason to jump too much in the warm-up.

Valentine jigged in place a few feet from the start box as they watched another horse head out on course. Her ears were zeroed in on the first jump the horse in the distance was taking, causing her to take a few steps forward again.

"Easy," Emma murmured, trying to calm the mare as she circled once more.

"You have thirty seconds," said the women with the stopwatch who stood next to the start box. Taking one large loop around the box, Emma walked her horse in just as they began counting down.

"Three...two...one...have a great ride!"

Valentine cantered off the moment her owner let the reins slide through her fingers, ears still pricked at the table in front of them. Her horse soared over it as they galloped on, taking the next few jumps with the same gung-ho approach as the first. Beaming now as they galloped across the open field towards the next jump some distance away, she felt her horse's muscles contracting and pushing them forward. It was the most exhilarating feeling she had ever felt; the thrill of competition mixed with the magic she had felt on cross country courses back at the farm. It was easy to forget this was the first time her horse had been on a cross country course competitively. It felt so natural as they left the ground again, clearing a brush box with room to spare.

"You know you are supposed to brush through the brush box," Emma said breathlessly as they headed toward the last few jumps on course. Checking her watch, she saw they had been going a little too fast and took the scenic route to the chevron. Turning towards the water complex, Emma kept her leg on, knowing her horse would probably hesitate at the head of the lake. Valentine trotted in reluctantly but picked up her pace when she saw the small up bank ahead that would take them out of the water.

Letting her horse roll out underneath her, they sailed over the final cross country jump, a roll top.

Checking her watch quickly as they landed, she gave Valentine's sweaty neck a much-deserved pat. They had another clear round under their belt for the day.

After Emma cooled and hosed her horse down, she sat in the grass as Valentine hand grazed lazily next to her. Michael sat a few feet away, and they chatted casually as they waited for the placings to be announced.

"Emma, the results are in," Lily said, a twinkle in her eye.

"I can't take the waiting anymore, Lil! How did we do today?" Emma pressed, standing up now.

"You and Nettie took second, Lenny was 8th, and Valentine placed 7th."

Emma looked over at her horse and smiled despite their less than ideal placing. For her first time at an eventing trial, she couldn't be too disappointed. It was no secret to her that dressage was going to be a work in progress, and at least now she knew what to work on at home.

Resting her chin on her mare's back, Emma patted the other side of her still damp barrel.

"We'll do better next time," she said softly.

Emma was sure that was true; this horse had nothing but heart.

Chapter Six

Emma pushed brush and low hanging branches aside as she walked through the tropical foliage that hung in the way of the path that led through the forest area across from her apartment.

These morning nature walks on her days off had become something she looked forward to as a way to decompress from a long work week. Sometimes she still showed up at Three Phases Farm to ride her own horse but taking a whole day away from the barn to just relax and unwind was something she found imperative from time to time.

She had discovered this little trail leading through a two-mile patch of forest one day while walking around the lake that lay behind her patio. She had noticed the break in the trees where the thin dirt path began and had decided to follow it. To her delight, Emma found it was longer than she expected, leading almost to the edge of the forest. Then, she would simply double back when she reached the end.

It wasn't much, but it was a long enough path that she could be alone in nature with her thoughts. Sometimes, she brought her headphones along to listen to some music as she walked along. Either way, these walks had become her day off ritual and had provided her with the same feeling of release that the walks around Twin Oaks Farm had provided.

As she walked toward the head of the path, she began feeling excitement about what today would bring. This was no ordinary day off lounging around in her pajamas like she normally would.

Today was the first day of looking at potential farms that Cathy was interested in purchasing.

To say this day had been something she had dreamed about would be an understatement. Since the moment Cathy mentioned the opportunity on the night of the Million Dollar Grand Prix, it had been in the back of her mind. Emma wondered what it would look like, or what it would be like moving into a place that would essentially be her forever home.

In a way, it had been bittersweet to think that as long as Cathy wanted her running the place, which at this point was indefinitely, that she knew exactly what her future career looked like. Of course, that seemed like a good thing, right? Knowing her future career wouldn't be in jeopardy the way it had in the past was a relief.

But the bitter part snuck up on her during one of these walks in the woods. In a way, she felt like her life was laid out in front of her, certain and steadfast. The mystery of what her life might look like was solidifying into a set path. Even her romantic life seemed to be falling into place; after all, Liam had made his feelings for her clear. Not that it solved any of their long-distance issues, but still, he seemed to want to work that out.

Sighing audibly, she mentally reprimanded herself for being so ungrateful. This is what she had wanted all along, wasn't it? Of course it was! She was being silly.

Excitement took the place of her anxious inner voice once again as she opened the door to her apartment. In a matter of an hour, she would be meeting Cathy and Liam at the first farm on their list of five farms they would be seeing today.

While Cathy planned to stay a few days to view more farms in case one of these five didn't work out, Liam planned to head back to Wellington in the morning so he could finish up some necessary work in order to prepare for an early meeting Monday morning. Emma was glad for the one day she would get to spend with him, although she knew it wouldn't feel like nearly enough by the time he left.

Emma hoped any lingering awkwardness that remained after her trip to Wellington a few weeks back would be ancient history now. Knowing Liam, he wouldn't bring up the conversation from the gala, and knowing herself, she wouldn't want to ruin such an important day for Cathy.

"Once again, we won't talk about the real issue," she thought.

In a way, it was a relief to know it wouldn't come back up. After all, once it did, they would have to deal with it like real adults, and that wasn't something she was ready to do if she was honest with herself.

"Ignorance is bliss," she thought as she changed into a new pair of jeans and a mint green top.

Emma pulled into the long driveway of a farm located on the outskirts of Ocala thirty minutes later. She saw Cathy's SUV parked just inside the gates and she and Liam were chatting with a slender man she assumed was the real estate agent.

"Emma, dear, it's so good to see you!" Cathy said, wrapping her arms around her the moment she stepped out of her car.

"Hey, Em," Liam said, pulling her in, kissing her quickly.

"This is our real estate agent," Cathy said, motioning toward the slender man.

"Jeff," said the man who had been standing next to them, offering his hand for Emma to shake.

"Shall we?" Jeff offered, leading the way towards the barn first. Emma watched Cathy's face fall as they got closer to the older, unstained wooden barn. She looked a little underwhelmed, and she wasn't wrong. While this barn was large and had ample stalls, it was certainly lacking the luster of the barns Emma had now become accustomed to in Ocala. Not to mention, the arena was incredibly small.

"The house is really what makes this property though," Jeff added quickly, reading their expressions.

"Jeff, perhaps I wasn't clear. I think we should stick to properties where the focus is on the equestrian facilities. Emma will be living onsite, but we are really looking for a working farm. Even if a house isn't included, we certainly want to look at some that could have a barn apartment added or small house if the barn meets our needs."

"This isn't going well already," Emma thought, worried about the rest of the list for the day. It made sense; Jeff probably assumed that with the caliber of client that Cathy was, a nicer house and mediocre barn would be what she was after. Knowing sweet Cathy, she probably hadn't spelled out exactly what she wanted the way she needed to. Liam had mentioned Aunt Cathy had owned her Wellington estate for a long time now and this was her first farm purchase.

"Emma, I think you may be the best person to discuss with Jeff about what it is we really need in a farm. Jeff, why don't you go over the list for today, and let's see what's left to look at that meets our requirements?"

Emma went through the list, looking at the descriptions he had listed next to each farm. She discovered that there was only one farm left on today's list that met their needs, but Jeff promised to find more for them to look at tomorrow that would be geared toward what they were looking for.

"Well, I suppose we can just head right to that property then," Cathy said, looking a touch disappointed. She had talked to Emma on the phone for almost an hour last night gushing with excitement about today's farm tours.

"Of course, follow me," Jeff said, heading back towards the parked cars. They drove fifteen minutes to the next property, and she already felt better about this one as they approached the gated entrance.

The large hunter green gates swung open, letting them catch the first glimpse of a dark stained barn sitting about an acre back from the entrance. It looked to be in good shape, and as they walked towards the barn's entrance a few moments later, she saw it had fifteen stalls, a wash rack, and two grooming bays.

"It certainly could use some new rubber mats and a really good cleaning, but I like it," Emma said to Cathy who was already opening every cabinet in the feed room. Liam trailed behind them, pretending to know what he was looking at as he peered into the stalls, glancing up at the rafters of the barn from time to time.

They headed to the back side of the property where three good sized pastures and a spacious outdoor arena were located. The property was very narrow, not nearly square shaped like Twin Oaks was, but still had the acreage and barn size which met their requirements.

"What do we think?" Jeff asked, meeting Cathy and Emma's gazes briefly, searching their eyes for approval. Emma couldn't find anything wrong with the farm, and it did meet their check-list items. Perhaps she was simply spoiled by Twin Oaks and Three Phases at this point, but there was something keeping her from wanting to tell Cathy this was the one.

"I like it," Emma said casually with a shrug.

"So do I," Cathy chimed in with the same lack of enthusiasm.

"I'll do some heavy research tonight and come up with some great options tomorrow. Cathy, I will send you the address of our first option, and we can meet there tomorrow morning."

"Thank you, Jeff," Cathy said as they headed back to the cars once again.

"You didn't love it, did you?" Cathy whispered to Emma as they walked.

"Oh, no, I mean it's a nice farm…," Emma said, trailing off as she searched for better words.

"Honey, it's fine. I didn't love it either. I just wanted to make sure I wasn't taking the option away from you if you did," Cathy replied.

Emma wasn't sure why she had imagined simply being a by-stander in the buying process of the farm. Emma knew Cathy well enough to know she would heavily involve her. But some-how, it felt like Cathy was buying this farm as much for Emma as herself. She wasn't sure if that was a good thing or a bad thing. It was certainly good in a sense that it was making her wildest career dreams come true.

"Is there really even a downside?" she thought.

Jeff pulled away in his car leaving Emma, Cathy, and Liam stand-ing by their cars.

"Alright, I'm sure you two want to catch up, so Liam why don't you just drop me by the hotel and you can meet up Emma for some quality time?" Cathy said with a wink to Emma, making her blush.

"I'll swing by your place after I drop off Aunt Cathy," Liam said, locking eyes with her for a moment.

"See you tomorrow, dear!" Cathy said to Emma before slipping into the car's passenger seat.

Emma waved before getting in her own car. Since she had the time, she decided to head the opposite direction of her apartment towards a very familiar place she hadn't been to in a few months now.

It had dawned on her when they arrived at this farm just how close they were to Twin Oaks. Driving down the familiar road, she remembered just how different her life had been the first time she had been on it. She certainly could have called Michael to let her in, who she suspected was watching TV in his trailer at this time of day, but in this moment, she just wanted to be alone.

Parking off the side of the road, Emma sat on the hood of her car staring over the fence line at the farm she once called home. She could barely make out the horses grazing in the nearest pasture, but that didn't really matter much. Emma didn't know why she was even here, why she suddenly felt so nostalgic. Although, she suspected the change in the air had a little something to do with it. After all, she was still a creature of habit who detested change deep down, even if that change was good. Plus, the breathtaking sunsets at Twin Oaks were something she had missed.

If anything, she was giving herself a chance to mentally prepare for being alone with Liam for the first time since her Wellington visit. It was another opportunity to discuss the subject neither of them wanted to address: what would their future look like?

Sitting there until the sun had disappeared behind the horizon, she finally pulled herself off her car's hood and slid back into the driver's seat.

At this point Liam was probably just now on his way to her place anyway.

She tossed the farm one last glance before pulling away toward route twenty-seven and her apartment.

Liam pulled into the parking spot next to her car moments after she arrived home, and she was still unlocking her front door when he got out of his car.

"Where were you?" he asked curiously, head tilted slightly to the side.

"I just wanted to watch the sunset, so I parked by Twin Oaks," Emma replied with a casual shrug.

"You didn't go in and see Michael or Jenn?" he asked, still prying.

"No, I didn't want to disturb anyone; I just felt like visiting the farm," Emma said.

"Are you having second thoughts about leaving Twin Oaks?" Liam asked, catching her hand as they walked into her apartment and locking eyes with her.

Of course she wasn't having second thoughts; running a farm for someone like Cathy was beyond a dream come true. Emma hoped Liam knew her well enough now to know she was simply processing the changes of the last couple months. In a way, she realized it wasn't his fault he didn't know this about her. After all, their relationship had begun strangely, and the whole stalker thing being thrown into the mix drew them close quickly without any solid foundation as friends.

"Not like the one Michael and I share," she thought, feeling a wave of guilt for even thinking that as she stood across from her boyfriend.

"I just have a hard time with change," Emma replied quietly, a sad half smile flashed across her face before she dropped her gaze.

"That makes sense. I understand," Liam said, as he wrapped his arms around her, pulling her in. "Why didn't you tell me before that's how you were feeling?" he added.

"I didn't want to say anything in front of Aunt Cathy. She has been crazy generous, and I don't want her thinking I'm ungrateful. Plus, it's not something that's easy to discuss over the phone; it just felt like more of an in-person thing to talk about," Emma replied.

"You know she loves you; I'm sure she would understand. You've had a lot of changes in a short amount of time. Anyone would feel a little strange adjusting to different places and circumstances. It hasn't even been a year since you left home in Ohio," Liam said.

It made her feel better that he seemed to understand where she was coming from. Liam was never one to judge her; he never had been.

"Thanks, and I'm glad you're here, especially now," she said, her eyes meeting his again.

"Of course. I just wish it was for more than a day," he replied.

Emma wanted to ask him when they'd see each other next but bit her tongue. Why ruin what little time they had left together tonight? It would only lead them back down the same road to the same conversation they had on the beach in Wellington.

"Want to watch a movie?" she asked with a playful grin on her face now, pulling him towards the couch.

"Sure," he said, smiling back with the goofy grin that had charmed her not so long ago.

Emma squealed as he tackled her onto the sofa, laughing as she sat back up. Fighting for the remote to prevent him from choosing his typical sports movie pick, he gave up willingly as she scrolled down to one of her favorite horse movies of all time.

"Ok, ok, but next time I pick," he teased, throwing his hands in the air in defeat. They sat close and she laid her head on his shoulder and closed her eyes as she held onto what she knew would be a fleeting moment.

Their future may still feel uncertain, but tonight, sitting next to him, she pretended none of that mattered.

elle

Dawn had barely cracked when Emma's alarm began chirping in her ear. Groaning, she turned it off but continued lying in bed with her eyes closed. It wasn't until her mind started turning over, reminding her of the day's events, that she finally opened her eyes a few minutes later.

Liam had left half an hour ago, halfway waking her up when he kissed her goodbye. She had drifted back off to sleep only ten minutes before her alarm had gone off. They had stayed up far too late watching movies, but despite how groggy she felt this morning, it had been worth spending that extra time together.

Rolling out of bed, she thanked herself for pre-prepping the coffee and setting the timer on the coffee maker. The smell of fresh brewed coffee wafting through the halls was motivation enough to stumble down the stairs.

Jeff had promised them a list of farms that would meet their expectations and had sent a few links to her and Cathy last night that made her excited for today. After the disappointing lineup yesterday, she hoped this time would be different based on the sneak preview she had seen.

Although, while she was excited that there was a very real possibility Cathy could choose to put an offer in on one of the farms from today's tour, she also knew that would mean she would be leaving Three Phases Farm. It had just begun to feel comfortable and familiar, and working alongside Lily was something she really enjoyed.

"You knew this was the plan all along," she reminded herself. Even this apartment she had all but scoffed at on moving day now felt like home. Her routine of walking around the lake and into the small forest were something she looked forward to now.

But she had promised herself and Liam she would focus on the good and keep that in the forefront of her mind as she transitioned once again to a new farm and home in the near future. Really, she should be used to change by now, shouldn't she?

After pulling on her favorite pair of jeans and a loose tank top, she headed to the coffee pot to fill her to-go cup. One cup of coffee wasn't going to cut it today, that much was clear. Slipping on her rubber boots, she headed to her car and down route twenty-seven towards the first farm on the list for the day.

Cathy greeted her with a wide smile and a kiss on the cheek when she arrived.

"Emma, you are going to love this place. I got a little excited and headed into the barn when I arrived early. Jeff, can you run through the specifics?"

"Sixteen stalls, about twenty acres...," Jeff began. Emma strode across the spongy grass with Cathy at her side as Jeff rattled off more facts about the property.

There was nothing she didn't like about the barn or the house on the property. The pastures and land were nice too, but it didn't have nearly as many trees scattered around the property like Twin Oaks or Three Phases. She didn't mean to, but it was hard not to compare every property they looked at to them. They spent nearly an hour looking at every detail of the property before moving on the next farm.

The next one was just as nice but was in a location that neither of them particularly liked. The neighbors on one side had land cluttered with old cars, and the neighbors on the other side of the farm looked like they hadn't mowed in months. That one was quickly crossed off their list.

The next two farms were also good prospects but did not have the same appeal as the first farm they had seen. That left just two more farms on today's list. Emma wondered if either of them would compare or if that first farm would be the winner. Jeff had mentioned if they absolutely didn't like these that he could keep digging, but odds were they would be out of Ocala in a surrounding town. Not that it would be the end of the world, but both Emma and Cathy wanted to stay in this central Ocala area they both loved so much.

Pulling into the gates of the second to last farm on the list, Emma couldn't park fast enough. Clutching her chest briefly after she scrambled from the car, she scanned the property twice almost in disbelief.

"There has to be something wrong with the inside of the barn," she thought.

There was no way this stunning property didn't have a major flaw hidden behind closed doors. Cathy put an arm around Emma's shoulders as her eyes also passed over the grounds, a similar look of awe crossing her face.

Endless rolling hills sprawled in every direction with scattered live oaks and the occasional palm tree dotted its landscape. There were four massive pastures that sat on either side of a natural wood barn with a natural stain, which she remembered reading was fifteen stalls. Behind the barn, in the back of the property, were several unfenced acres of green space that Emma could easily picture being the perfect place for cross country jumps. One large sand ring sat between the barn and the empty unfenced green space, and it looked like an apartment was recently built above the barn. A small, newer looking house sat at the front of the property.

They still had not uttered a word, but walked towards the barn, pushing open the sliding door. It was a little older than some of the others, but well maintained. With a bit of cleaning and a few minor updates, Emma imagined just how nice it could be. The stalls were open air style, and a hay loft above ran along the left side of the barn. On the right by the entrance was the door leading to a small feed room, hay room, and a moderate sized tack room. Perhaps a little smaller than Twin Oaks had been, but perfect for the operation they would be running. There were two grooming bays at the end of the aisle and an outdoor wash rack behind the barn, on the side where the arena was.

"Shall we take a look at the apartment upstairs? We can head over to the house after that," Jeff said, motioning them back outside and towards the staircase on the side of the barn. The barn apartment ran the length of the barn below it and had a light wood throughout on the walls and floor. It had a small kitchenette, and a newer looking couch with a small TV stand were in the main room. The bedroom was a separate room with a simple bed, nightstand, and dresser setup.

If the property had not come with a house as well, Emma knew this would have been her home. Honestly, she would probably have still loved this place just as much even if that was the case.

Jeff led the way back down the stairs and across the lawn towards the small house. He talked along the way, mentioning it had only been built as an add-on five years ago. The previous owners lived in the barn apartment and just had their own private horses here, only staying in Ocala four or five months out of the year for the winter show season. The house was a dark grey with white trim and had stones lining the flower bed that ran on either side of the front of the house.

"The house is about 1,800 square feet including the finished basement, with two bathrooms," Jeff stated as he opened the door for them. Emma looked around the cozy living room which had some grey wood looking porcelain tile running throughout. Three large windows lined the back wall of the living room and the kitchen had black countertops and white cabinets. They walked down the hallway, peeking in the two bedrooms upstairs which were moderate in size. Leading the way down the staircase at the end of the hall, they stepped into a spacious finished basement that had another separate bedroom and living room space along with its own bathroom. Since the house was built on a slight hill, there were windows in the basement and a door leading to the back of the house.

"This would be the perfect place for me to stay when I'm in town, so I can still stay out of your hair," Cathy commented.

Emma tossed a surprised look to Cathy.

"Cathy, this is *your* property. You can stay wherever you want!"

"I know, honey, but I want this to be your home. I have a house that's far too big in Wellington, so I certainly don't need this as well," Cathy said, motioning to the walls around them.

They stepped outside using the basement door and made their way back around to the front of the house. The view from where they stood gave them a glimpse of everything the gorgeous property had to offer.

"It's perfect," Emma muttered to herself as she stepped back outside, staring out at the Spanish moss blowing in the light breeze.

Cathy looked over at her, following her gaze. With an all-knowing smile, she turned back to the real estate agent.

"Jeff dear, I'm not sure looking at that final property will be necessary. Emma, what do you think?"

"I think it's everything I could have imagined and then some. But Cathy, this is your farm so if you want to keep looking, I would be fine with...," Emma began.

Cathy waved her hand in the air, cutting her off.

"Nonsense, dear. I was already in love with it the moment we pulled in and the look of wonder on your face as you looked around, well, that was all I needed to make my decision. Jeff, can you please draw up the paperwork? You can speak with my financial advisor with any questions about the offer amount," Cathy stated, turning to Jeff.

Jeff looked all but giddy, nodding to Cathy. "Of course, ma'am, I will be in touch regarding the next steps," he said.

Surely, he was in for one heck of a payday considering the price tag on this property. Jeff walked to his car where he would, most likely, head to his office to begin the process of putting an offer in for Cathy's soon-to-be farm.

Emma still had not peeled her eyes from the horizon of the farm, and she was envisioning what it would look like with a pink-orange watercolor painted sky behind it. Cathy pulled a handkerchief from her pocket, dabbing her eyes.

"I can't thank you enough for this," Emma said, still scanning the property around them.

"You know you're making my dreams come true too, right? I couldn't do this without you. I couldn't have dreamed of buying this place and entrusting it to anyone else. I know my horses and the staff we hire will be in good hands with you my dear," Cathy said.

Emma could only hope she would live up to Cathy's words.

Chapter Seven

Valentine trotted down the long side of the dressage ring at Three Phases Farm, her back still much more tense than Emma preferred.

This mare's trot was night and day after she had cantered versus before. It was as if she was thinking, "Ok, we already cantered so what's the point in trotting again when we could be cantering still or jumping?" Every other stride Emma felt the mare almost break back into the canter.

Of course, the glaring problem here is dressage tests require you to trot after you've cantered, much to Valentine's dismay. Emma sat as lightly as possibly as she posted along, hoping her soft, wide contact in the reins and slow posting would relax her horse's still tense back.

Coming down the center line she halted her horse, focusing on keeping the mare as straight as possible. They stood there a few extra moments so that her horse wouldn't get in the bad habit of walking off two seconds after they halted.

Patting her horse, she looked up to see Michael hanging his arms over the gate, staring at them from under his ball cap. She hadn't even noticed him standing there, or how long ago he arrived, since she had been so focused on her horse.

"Hey, you!" Michael called out when she met his gaze.

"Hey! I hope I haven't kept you waiting long; Val has been a little fireball today," she said, rolling her eyes but smiling at the mare anyway. Even on her spiciest day, she couldn't stay mad at her horse for very long.

"She does look like a ticking timebomb today," he said with a deep laugh as he patted Valentine's sweaty neck.

"That's because she is. I could not get her to relax at the trot after cantering to save my life. It's not usually this bad, but today was a little cooler than usual so she has been fiery. I think she's in heat too," Emma said, shaking her head.

Michael laughed again, watching Valentine power walk across the grassy area behind the arena as Emma lapped the ring in an attempt to walk her out.

"You know you're never going to cool out when you are walking that fast, right?" Emma said to the mare whose left ear swiveled back, listening to her owner but making no attempt to slow her pace.

"Sorry Michael, it looks like I'm going to need to walk her out in the field to get her mind off the arena work and cool her jets a little bit. I'll be back in ten," she said, turning around in the saddle as her mare powered forward into the open field.

Normally, once she was a little farther from the arena, her mare started to relax her body and take a deep breath.

"Today, however, may be a different story," she thought. It was always the days she had plans and needed to be somewhere that things seemed to go wrong with horses.

"It's like they know," she thought.

Her horse finally settled into a regularly-paced, slow walk and just over ten minutes later she was able to head back to the barns and dismount.

"Want some help untacking so we can head out?" Michael asked as she slid off Valentine's side.

"Sure, that would be great, thanks!" Emma replied.

Emma led her horse back into the now quiet barn. Lily had stopped by the ring to say goodbye to her before heading to an early happy hour with a guy she had just started seeing. Emma couldn't help but notice the mischievous glimmer in her friend's eye when Lily told her to have a safe trip and to let her know how it went with Michael. It made her *almost* regret telling her about the kiss. Had Emma not been in the middle of an intense ride on her mare, she would have been sure to offer a quick-witted comment about how it wasn't a big deal and they were simply carpooling to an event they both happened to be attending.

Michael slid Valentine's bridle off and replaced it with her halter as Emma pulled the saddle off and headed to the tack room. She heard her mare's hooves clinking against the concrete as he led her horse to the wash bay, followed by the sound of the hose water splashing against the wall. It reminded her of old times back when they still worked together at Twin Oaks.

Emma had been looking forward to spending some extended time on this road trip with her best friend since they hadn't been able to see each other in person more than once a week lately.

"Is Valentine getting turned out tonight?" Michael called from the wash rack after she heard the squeaky sound of the water being turned off.

"Yes, the first pasture across from barn one. Thanks!" Emma replied as she finished wiping down her tack, twisting her bridle into a neat figure eight. Emma braided her long, thick hair into a side braid and placed a ball cap on her head.

"Good enough. It's a horse event after all," she thought.

By the time Michael had returned from turning Valentine out, Emma was pulling her overnight bag and purse from her car.

"Ready to go?" he asked, opening the passenger side of the Twin Oaks truck for her.

"Ready!" she said enthusiastically as she climbed in, throwing her bag in the truck bed.

The familiar truck rolled down the back roads towards the highway, and Emma felt the excitement of the evening start to creep in.

"So, it's about two and a half hours to the competition, right?" she asked, turning her head from the window to look over at him.

"Yeah, about that long, not including stops. By the way, Jenn was excited to hear you were coming up to watch Jimmie John compete tonight. I'm no expert on Grand Prixes, but she made it sound like this was one was a big deal," Michael replied.

"That's because it is a big deal," Emma said, chuckling a little as she spoke.

When Michael had mentioned the out-of-town show to her and asked if she had wanted to come along, she had immediately said yes. How could she pass up an opportunity to watch a horse she loved like her own compete at such a prestigious event? Plus, seeing some of her old coworkers and spending time with Michal made it that much more appealing. Although, Lily had teased her about it being an overnight event.

"The show starts in the evening and runs late. This is such a cool location right on the coast, so it just makes sense to make a night of it and come back home the next morning," Emma had told Lily with a bit of a defensive tone. Lily wasn't actually implying anything of course, but her knowing their secret had made Emma a little defensive, nonetheless.

"So, tell me about this new farm you and Cathy found last week. I know you mentioned it was officially under contract, but I want details," he said with a boyish grin.

"Michael, I can't wait to show you this place. It literally took my breath away," Emma replied, her voice reflecting her excitement about the farm.

Emma continued to gush, going over every detail about her future farm.

"We are still working out the details of the closing date, but it looks like within a couple months we'll be moving in. It's still a little surreal, you know? Running my own farm...," she paused, shaking her head in disbelief. "Well it's not something I dreamed would ever happen for me, especially this soon. Meeting Cathy was like some crazy twist of fate I never expected," Emma said.

"I hope you know I'm proud of you, and I think you will do amazing. You've come a long way from the person you were your first day at Twin Oaks," Michael replied.

It felt good to know that Michael was in her corner still, and that he believed in her. Looking back out the window as trees on the side of the highway blurred by, she considered just how smart her decision had been to move to Florida. It had been so hard, but if she could talk to her past self, she would tell her it was all worth it in the end. Sometimes she wondered what her life would have been like if she had never left home or even if she had been able to finish college in the first place. She had been so directionless in school, assuming things would fall into place on their own. Younger, naïve Emma didn't realize that is not how the real adult world works.

Certainly, she wouldn't be the person she was today without the kick in the rear end that figuring out life without a college degree had been.

They pulled into the elaborate show grounds a couple hours later, just as the sun was setting. Emma could see the bright flood lights in the arena peeking out from atop the bleachers as they walked from the back of the packed parking lot. A tingle of excitement spread through her as they reached the warm-up ring.

There, she saw Jimmie John cantering boldly toward a warm-up fence, floating over it with his typical ease. He shook his head as he landed, as if to say, "That was easy; can someone raise the jumps a little?"

She watched as Jenn circled the warm-up ring, waiting for one of the higher jumps to be free. Calling it out, she pointed Jimmie, who eagerly leaped over the ramped oxer enthusiastically. Turning him on his haunches, Jenn rolled back, and the dark bay gelding took the massive fence beside it with similar gusto. She slowed him to a walk, patting his neck.

Emma waved from the side of the warm-up ring and Jenn waved back, smiled when she spotted them and headed their way.

"Emma! I'm so glad you could come out tonight. I'm sure Jimmie is happy to see one of his favorite people too, aren't you buddy?" Jenn said, looking down at the gelding.

Emma reached over the fence and ran her fingers up his forelock. Scratching his neck in his favorite place, the gelding tilted his head, leaning into her hand.

"I missed you too, Jimmie," she said with a laugh as she continued scratching.

"I better keep this guy walking, but stop by and say hi after?" Jenn asked them.

"Definitely," Emma replied. Jenn walked the gelding off, and Michael turned to meet Emma's gaze.

"Shall we?" he asked, pulling out the tickets and waving them in the air before offering for her to loop her arm into his.

"We shall!" she replied, and he led them toward the grand-stands.

The first rider was due to go on course any minute and there was a buzz of energy in the crowd she had long missed.

"It is nice to be a spectator once and awhile," she thought.

They slid into their seats just as the announcer's voice broke the silence, echoing the rider and horse's name. She felt nervous even though she wasn't the one in the saddle as the horse before Jimmie John entered the ring. She had pressed Michael for details about how Jimmie had been doing in training and in some of the schooling competitions he had been in since she left Twin Oaks, but poor Michael's answers had not been as in depth as she had preferred.

The horse on course took down two rails and was exiting the ring as Emma saw Jimmie entering the arena with his typical swagger. He jigged in place, ears forward as he waited for the sound he knew all too well.

The buzzer sound made her own heart skip a beat, and Jenn asked him to canter forward. Watching Jimmie fly over the first few fences, she could already see the improvement in his form over these Grand Prix level fences. His focus was only on the jumps in front of him, despite the crowd and distractions he had once succumbed to during his first few competitions at this level.

Jimmie had more scope than most horses she had met, and he was clearing every fence he had taken so far with room to spare. Taking a deep spot to the two-stride line, she watched as Jenn legged him up to the second fence of the combination with Jimmie responding effortlessly.

They approached the final fence, a wide oxer, and Emma found herself standing up as she cheered on the pair. As Jimmie landed on the other side, he shook his head, galloping off exuberantly. Sometimes she swore he understood that his job was to leave the rails up and seemed pleased with himself when he did.

Looking over she saw Michael was on his feet too cheering just as loudly for Jimmie and Jenn. She didn't know why she was a little surprised to see that he seemed to be enjoying himself almost as much as she was. After all, he loved horses too.

It was part of the reason his friendship was so invaluable to her. She didn't mean to think it, but it was the one thing she wished Liam shared with her too.

"Of course he likes horses too," she thought, mentally scolding herself for comparing what she and Michael shared with her relationship with Liam. Liam was supportive of her and his aunt's love of horses, but did he like them per se? That she couldn't truly answer. If she and Cathy both one day woke up and decided they no longer wanted to be involved with horses, Liam probably wouldn't be all that upset about it.

Shaking her head to clear her mind of things she had no business dwelling on, she slipped out of the grandstands with Michel close behind her as they headed to the exit gate Jimmie had just made his way to.

The dark bay was breathing heavily as they approached, but he had a glimmer in his eye and jigged like he could lap the course again if Jenn asked him.

"Jenn, he has come such a long way since I last saw him go around a course. He looks amazing! It's no surprise you had a clear round," Emma said, patting his neck.

"Thanks, Em, we have been working hard to get him ready for an event of this caliber, but as usual he impressed me. He really gave me his all out there," Jenn said, beaming.

"I'll let you get him cooled out, but make sure you give him a cookie for me," Emma said, rubbing the gelding behind the ears once more.

"I sure will, and congrats on the new farm by the way! Stop by Twin Oaks soon, ok?" Jenn said warmly before walking away.

"I will, thanks!" Emma called after them.

They headed back to the grandstands after that, and watched the remaining horses go around the course so they could hear how Jimmie placed.

"…and in third place is Freaky Fast owned by the Twin Oaks Syndicate," the announcer stated after a short intermission.

Emma turned to Michael, eyes wide and grinning broadly.

"That's incredible! Third place for a competition like this?" Emma was shaking her head now almost in disbelief.

"He's a special guy, isn't he?" Michael said, chiming in. "Ready to head out? I have a surprise for you," he added.

"Is that so? I take it you're not going to tell me where we are going to dinner then?" Emma said, sounding intrigued.

"Nope, that's part of the surprise!" Michael said, shooting her a look that said he wasn't going to give her any hints.

Emma shot him a teasing glare back, but internally, she was excited for whatever he had cooked up. Michael drove about twenty minutes from the horse show grounds before parking in a lot behind a side street.

"Where are we?" Emma asked, peering out the window at a parking lot that was pitch black other than one streetlight.

"You'll see, come on," he said with a sneaky smile.

They walked side by side down the dark side street that led from the parking lot to what looked like a more main street. It was dotted with restaurants and beach themed shops, but she almost didn't notice any of that at first because something else had drawn her attention.

"Is that the ocean?" Emma asked, pointing across the street at the empty blackness behind a short fence surrounded by tall beach grass. Had the tufts of beach grass not been visible by the streetlamps, she still would have known it was out there somewhere in the dark. The wind rushing off the ocean was always unmistakable to her, but not just that, she swore she could smell it.

"You're like an ocean bloodhound," he teased, laughing deeply. "But yes, you are right." She had mentioned more than once that she could smell the ocean before she saw it.

"This way," he motioned as they crossed the street. The restaurant ahead of them was set directly on the pier that overlooked the water.

"Michael, this place is perfect!" she said, eyes wide as she took in the view.

"Before you say anything, I called ahead and made sure we have a view of the water outside, even if it's too dark to see much of anything," Michael added lightly.

"Yep, you know me too well," Emma replied, still grinning as they were seated on the deck area.

After she spent far too long deciding what she wanted to eat, they placed their orders and sipped the margaritas the waitress brought them.

"Just like old times," she said, holding up their favorite drink of choice whenever they went out to eat together.

"Cheers," he added, clinking his glass against hers.

Emma stared out at the dark water, marveling at the tide going in and out in the dim lights on the pier.

"I'm glad you like it," he stated, and she felt his eyes on her as she was staring out at the water.

"Really, Michael, this was incredibly thoughtful. Thanks again for bringing me here," Emma said softly.

"Of course, I'm glad it made you happy," Michael said, and Emma could still feel his eyes on her.

Emma wanted to pretend she hadn't seen it, but the way he looked at her when she caught his face in her peripherals was something she had seen once before. It was the way he had looked at her just before he kissed her. Was she really that blind? Had she avoided the very real possibility he harbored feelings for her this whole time because of the tension she knew it would cause between them and in her relationship with Liam?

To be fair, he had said twice that the kiss meant nothing, and that it was an alcohol-induced mistake.

"Don't overreact, it was just a look," she told herself.

Perhaps it was, but she couldn't deny that maybe now she would be observing the way Michael interacted with her a little more closely. Regardless, she wasn't going to ruin this night with sneaky suspicions of feelings Michael may or may not have for her. Even if he did, he clearly wasn't going to act on them. Michael was a gentleman at his core, and a good person; he wouldn't make the same mistake twice.

"So, tell me everything that has happened at Twin Oaks since I left," Emma said, changing the subject on her mind.

Michael went on about how Jenn and the Williams were doing, adding in a funny story about how Mateo had been drug into a mud puddle by one of the new young, green prospects that just came in. They continued to chat and reminisce about their time together at Twin Oaks, and how the Williams were beginning their search for next season's working student.

It felt a little bit strange to think someone would be taking her place there and sleeping in the guesthouse she once called home. This new girl would be working side by side with Michael too. What she hadn't expected was a twinge of jealously that brought, some new girl potentially taking her place as Michael's friend and confidant at work.

There had not been a moment until now that had rocked her confidence in their friendship until she considered that she could potentially be replaced. Of course, Michael was hardly a social butterfly with people he didn't know well; she had learned that firsthand when she first arrived at Twin Oaks.

Still, she couldn't shake feeling that there was a real possibility the friendship they shared was somehow threatened by this future working student, however silly she knew it was to feel that way.

The clang of a fork hitting Michael's now empty plate pulled her from her thoughts.

"Do you want a to-go box?" he said, eyeing her half-eaten dinner.

"Sure, thanks," she replied.

He waved down the waitress, paid the tab, and retrieved a box for her remaining dinner. They headed out of the restaurant a little while later, and Emma enjoyed the short walk down the coastal road back to the truck.

The hotel was only ten minutes from where they had dinner, and Emma suddenly felt the exhaustion of the day hit her as they pulled their luggage down the hall towards the rooms they had booked.

"This is me," Michael said, pausing at a hotel door.

"I think I'm two doors down," Emma said, looking at her key card once more to confirm.

They paused, holding each other's gaze for a few seconds before Michael stepped across the hall into her personal space.

"Today was fun," he murmured. His arm's wrapped around her back, pulling her to his chest briefly.

As they were pulling away, they locked gazes again. Emma peeled her eyes away quickly. She was afraid if she stared into his green eyes too long, she was going to see something behind them she couldn't unsee. Especially since she already had her suspicions about his true feelings for her.

"Goodnight, Michael." she offered with a quick smile before turning to head farther down the hall so he wouldn't think anything was amiss.

"Night, Em," he called after her, his tone giving away a hint of surprise at the way she had so abruptly turned on her heels.

Emma unlocked the door to her hotel room and leaned against the back of the door, closing her eyes as she did.

She hated the guilt that always seemed to find her every time she and Michael spent one on one time together. It was as if the kiss still hung over their heads, or that she felt like she was somehow cheating on Liam, which she was not. Emma was not that kind of girl.

Emma wondered if they were ever really going to move past this or if she was doomed to have her friendship with Michael muddled with a one-time mistake.

The alternative, which was choosing between the two of them, was an alternative she still couldn't fathom.

Letting her body flop onto the hotel bed, she dialed Liam's number in hopes of easing the guilt. Emma had mentioned going to the show and she had mentioned that Michael would be here too but had been a little vague about the rest of the details. Honestly, she didn't even know why. He probably wouldn't have cared that they had carpooled since he liked Michael, and Emma knew there was only one way to keep it that way: keep the kiss a secret.

"Hey babe, you're up late," Liam said, sounding tired.

"Sorry, did I wake you?" Emma replied softly.

"It's ok, I just have an early meeting tomorrow. Everything ok?"

"Everything is fine. I just got back to the hotel from the show."

"Oh, that's right, Jimmie John was competing out of town today, wasn't he?"

"Yep, that's the one."

"Do you mind if we talk about it tomorrow?" Liam said, yawning as he spoke.

"Of course, just call me tomorrow," Emma replied.

"I will, night Em, love you," Liam added, making it feel like someone had punched her in the gut.

"You too, night," she said, quickly hanging up.

"You too? Ugh!" she thought. Groaning, she rolled back over and headed to the bathroom, splashing water on her face before she crawled back into bad.

Flipping on the TV, she lay there another two hours praying sleep would find her.

Instead, her mind continued turning over the same facts that had been haunting her for months now.

___ele___

"That's great Emma, keep her balanced and straight," Ben David called from the other end of the Three Phases Farm arena.

Emma put her inside leg on the young, green mare she was riding, steadying her outside rein and the horse responded to her aids.

"Good, just like that!" Ben called out again as she completed a twenty-meter circle.

Emma was glad that Ben had offered to come by the new farm once a week until they would be able to find a permanent trainer, because the improvement she had seen in her own riding these past few months at his farm had been invaluable.

It was hard to believe that they were only weeks away from closing on this new farm. Cathy had asked her to start thinking of a list of potential farm names and to send her the top three.

Right now, that list was still completely blank. Of course, she planned on sitting down at some point to brainstorm, but she had simply been too busy or made excuses lately for that to actually happen. Now that the timeclock was ticking, she felt this pressure to soak up every ounce of training and experience she could from this farm before she was in charge of one herself.

"Good work today, Emma, go ahead and walk her out," Ben said as he headed out of the arena. Loosening the reins, Emma walked the mare out of the ring towards the open pasture she preferred to walk the horses out in.

It had been two weeks since the trip she took with Michael and since then, she had only seen him once. Of course, she had blamed being too busy trying to gain necessary experience and other things involved with the upcoming farm move, and Michael seemed to have bought it. Deep down though, she had been subconsciously keeping him at arm's length. Emma knew it was stupid, and only hurting their friendship unnecessarily, but she felt like at this point with all the other changes in her life that she needed to focus on one thing at a time.

"Maybe I'll call him after work and plan something," she thought as the horse under her walked across the spongy grass.

At least things between her and Liam seemed to be going well for now. Maybe taking a few weeks to focus on her relationship with him and everything she needed to prepare for the big move was a good idea after all. Still, she couldn't help the pang of feeling like something was missing without talking to or seeing Michael like she was used to.

Lily was standing in front of the barn holding the reins in one hand to her horse, Annie, who was fully tacked up, as well as a tacked up Valentine in the other.

"What's all this, Lil?" Emma said, tilting her head curiously. She was racking her brain for plans they may have had that had perhaps been drowned out by her own inner turmoil and hectic schedule.

"This is a kidnapping. You have been all kinds of stressed for weeks and while you may not be ready to talk about it, we are about to go on a conditioning gallop that's sure to clear your head," Lily said with a wink.

"Is it that obvious?" Emma said with a heavy sigh as she slid off the young mare's side. She had not been in the mood to talk in depth with Lily or anyone else really in the past weeks but hadn't realized just how outwardly her inner stresses had been showing.

"Thank God for Lily," she thought. Bottling everything up clearly wasn't getting her anywhere, and Lily was the kind of friend ready to call her out on it.

"Before you give me the excuse about needing to untack the horse you just rode, Hank is on his way to take her to be hosed down for you, and he has been instructed not to take no for an answer," Lily added, smiling confidently, clearly proud of her meddling.

"Ok, you win, I will go hand her off to Hank...," she cut herself off, seeing Hank emerge from the barn halfway through her sentence.

"I got her Emma," Hank said with his usual warm smile.

"Thank you, Hank," she said, returning his warm smile with one of her own.

"Mount up sister," Lily said, tossing her horse's reins at Emma.

Emma led Valentine to the mounting block and Lily followed suit. The young women followed the dirt path that led to the beginning of the galloping path which allowed the perfect amount of time to warm up at the walk and trot before it was time to open the horses up.

"Ready?" Lily said, giving Emma a mischievous look when they had reached the beginning of the galloping path. Before she had a chance to answer, Lily made a kissing sound to Annie, who responded immediately by galloping off. Valentine danced, chomping at the bit as she watched her horse friend gallop away from her.

Laughing for the first time in far too long, Emma released the reins and her horse followed after Annie, tearing up the ground under them as she charged down the horse in front of them.

The wind howling in her ears was only drowned out by the sound of pounding hooves under her and beside her now as they kept pace with Lily's horse. It was as if the entire world as she knew it melted away, and the only thing left was the ground beneath and the sky above. It had always been this way when she was able to let a horse really open up and gallop with nothing ahead of them but miles of land. It was something that happened even in her younger years where the stresses of life were much different, but still present, nonetheless. She remembered taking Lexington, her first horse, out to the back pasture at Maggie's to just let him loose and gallop until they ran out of land. Emma imagined this is what it felt like to fly, although to her, this was better. The connection with her horse as they moved as one flying across the open field couldn't possibly be trumped by actually flying in her opinion.

It was a moment just like this that her mind had become perfectly clear when she had decided to set aside her past heartbreak of losing Lexington to buy Valentine. That had been one of the best decisions she had ever made. Valentine had saved her both mentally and psychically. Valentine had given Emma the strength to move a thousand miles from home, knowing that even if she didn't know a single human, she had her horse.

"We can do anything together, you and I," she had whispered that complicated night after the Million Dollar Grand Prix. Was that not still true? She had so many good things in her life right now, things Emma would have given anything for at one point in her past.

They had only been galloping down this path for maybe three minutes, but it was like someone hit the slow-motion button on the world. In those few minutes, Emma gained the clarity and perspective she needed and a peace that followed because of it. They slowed back to a walk shortly after, both girls and horses breathed heavily.

"You're a genius Lily, that's exactly what I needed," Emma said, still a little breathless.

"It's what always helps me too," Lily said with a half shrug.

"I don't know how I managed to get myself so wound up lately. I guess just so much happening at once, and so much change,"

Emma replied, shaking her head in disbelief. How had she managed to let herself get into this mental state in the first place?

The girls walked along quietly for a while, taking in the cool of the evening and the birds chirping nearby. Emma would miss being on the same farm as Lily, despite how excited she was about the new farm.

"Want to help me come up with a name?" Emma asked. She figured while her mind was clear, it was the ideal time to brainstorm.

"I would be honored," Lily said, looking over at her with a soft look in her eye. The women tossed around a few names that felt either wrong or too weird.

"What about High Hill Farm because of all the pretty rolling hills it has?" Lily suggested.

"That sort of reminds me of Highpoint Stables which, obviously has a connection with Bo and that whole incident," Emma said, cringing a little at the memory.

"Yikes, we don't want that. Ok, automatically vetoed," Lily agreed.

They walked on, brainstorming in silence. Emma's eyes scanned the path ahead of them that wound around the cross country field. This was her favorite part of the path, not just because it had a killer view of the cross country course, but because it was heavily dotted with the live oaks covered in Spanish moss that she loved so much.

A short gasp escaped her the moment the thought popped it her mind.

"Lily, I think I have it," Emma said, turning in the saddle to face her friend. Lily turned around quickly, staring wide-eyed at Emma until she answered.

"Live Oaks Farm," Emma said proudly. Perhaps it was a touch cliché in a sense, and she was not immune to the fact it had a very similar name to Twin Oaks, but it was the perfect name in her mind for so many reasons. Emma had been instantly drawn to the live oaks and their Spanish moss that hung from them since the day she arrived in Florida. It was her favorite part of Ocala's landscape, and it had been a huge part of what made their new farm so magical to her.

"Em, I think it's perfect," Lily said, following Emma's gaze to the very trees that had triggered the idea.

"Hopefully Cathy won't mind the fact that this list is going to consist of only one name," she thought. Although, she highly doubted Cathy would give her any push back on it, especially once Emma explained her connection with the name. Cathy had made it clear that she wanted Emma heavily involved in everything about this new farm venture.

There just wasn't a name she could possibly find more fitting. Now that the farm had a name, it felt all the more real.

"This is really happening," she thought as they continued walking towards the setting sun.

—ele—

The tires on Emma's car crunched against the dried foliage that lay in the driveway at Live Oaks Farm.

Emma's car windows were rolled all the way down as she enjoyed what was turning out to be a gorgeous day.

"This place is going to need a landscaper," said Cathy, who was standing next to her own car, looking around the entrance of the property.

"Curb appeal is everything," Cathy added, waving her hand towards the half dead bushes that lined the entrance near the gate.

Emma wasn't particularly picky about that kind of thing, but this time, Cathy wasn't wrong. While the barn and house were well kept, the owners of this farm had done nothing in the way of landscaping at the entrance, or really anywhere else on the property for that matter. Since they had used the farm for a seasonal property for their own horses, they clearly hadn't felt the need to do landscaping.

"I'm sure the interviewees will understand," Emma replied as she approached Cathy, whose hands were now on her hips with a concerned look on her face.

"Let's hope so. I want the best staff we can possibly hire for this place," Cathy added, smiling with her eyes at Emma this time.

"We will, don't worry," Emma reassured Cathy, resting her hand on her shoulder. Throughout the process of buying this farm, Cathy had not seemed terribly unsettled about anything until now. It was clear to Emma how important it was to hire the right people. If there had ever been a moment Emma had wondered if she had only been chosen to run this farm because she was dating her nephew, those lingering doubts had vanished recently. In a way, it made sense why Cathy had chosen her to run this place. She seemed to mean what she said; she wanted people she could trust.

Cathy had called last night to go over the list of staff they would be interviewing today and the positions they planned to hire for now, stating they would add to their team as needed down the road.

They would not have too many horses at first; Valentine, of course, and when Lily went to college in the fall, she also planned to board her horse here since she was only going to be working part-time with Ben David and wouldn't be able to afford board at Three Phases Farm since she was losing the full-time employee discount. Cathy and Emma had both eagerly agreed to help her out since Lily would be providing most of the care and feed for Annie.

Cathy had also spoken to some contacts in the eventing world, putting the word out that they would be offering board to a few select people. Cathy had mentioned that she wanted to start boarding only a handful of horses at first and work their way up to a maximum of seven or eight boarders, leaving plenty of room for project sale horses and her own personal horses. Cathy had mentioned that Emma should consider purchasing a second young prospect that was all her own once they closed on the farm, since there would always be stalls reserved for Emma's horses. For that, she had felt both excited and grateful. Valentine would always be safe and have a home, and she would have a young prospect that would surely be moving up the levels by the time Val needed to retire.

So far, Cathy had three boarders lined up to move into the farm shortly after they took possession. The landscape not being up to Cathy's standard certainly had something to do with impressing these new boarders as well.

"Cathy, I don't think you told me who we will be putting in the apartment above the barn." Emma stated.

Cathy spun around, with a secretive smile. "Don't worry about that, I actually have someone in mind. I spoke to him earlier this week and he has tentatively accepted the position. I think you'll approve though," she added.

"Oh, I didn't realize you hired anyone already. Will I meet him today?"

"He plans to stop by later today since he hasn't officially seen the property yet," Cathy added, turning to walk towards the barn.

Emma was a little nervous about who she would be sharing the property with, especially since she had assumed it would be someone she would be interviewing today. But, if Cathy liked and trusted whoever this was, she was sure they would be a good fit. Perhaps it was even better that it was someone that Cathy seemed to know already.

"How's Liam?" Emma asked as they walked towards the barn. He had come up once last week to spend the day with her, but they had both been busy since then and hadn't had much time to talk.

"Oh, you know, his job keeps him busy, but he sends his love dear. Of course, he will be helping us during move-in week; I made sure he took time off work for that. Speaking of, I ordered all your furniture for the house, so all you need to do is go pick out your bedding and décor," Cathy replied.

It was still surreal this beautiful place would soon be her home. Cathy had asked Emma what kind of furniture she wanted, but home design had never really been her thing. Cathy had eagerly taken the opportunity to pick out furniture for her and run with it.

"You're the best, I'm sure whatever you picked out is going to look amazing in that house," Emma said.

Before Cathy could answer, a truck pulled through the gates of the farm.

"Ah, there is our first interview!" Cathy said, excitement clear in her voice. Emma glanced down at the list they had pre-made so they could remember who they were interviewing when.

"This is Travis Warner; he is interviewing for the general farm worker position," Emma stated.

They waited for the interview to park before making their way to greet him and escort him to the barn to show him around. Sitting down at the table and chairs they had set up in the aisleway, Emma and Cathy took turns asking their interview questions.

"So, your resume says you worked at your last farm for about a year? Can you tell us why you are leaving them?" Cathy asked, her eyes running up and down the resume in her hand.

"I just didn't really like it there," Travis said with a half shrug. Emma glanced over at Cathy who was never one to hide her true emotions. Sure enough, a quick look of distaste crossed her face. Emma jumped back in with another question, hoping to distract Travis from Cathy's expression.

"And can you tell us a little bit about your daily tasks?" Emma asked him. Travis rattled off a list of basic farm tasks, and Cathy began looking more unimpressed as each minute passed.

"Thank you for your time, Travis. We will be in touch," Cathy said politely as they wrapped up the interview.

When he was safely in his car, Emma glanced over at Cathy.

"Hard pass?" Emma asked in a teasing tone.

"You got that right," Cathy said, turning back toward the table to review the list.

They only had a few others left for the day, all of which were general farm help. Emma would of course be the barn's manger, but hiring a trainer had been a much harder process than they had originally anticipated, and the only one they found that was qualified couldn't come out to interview today. Cathy had said she wasn't too worried; hiring a trainer was one of the most important parts of starting up this new farm and may take time. Plus, Ben David had agreed to continue to train Emma and their horses until they found a permanent person. Cathy had already mentioned Emma was more than qualified to work with the prospects they would be purchasing and exercise boarders' horses for as long as that took.

"At least there won't be many horses on the farm at first," Emma thought.

The next two interviews went better than the first, reviving Cathy's enthusiasm. Neither stood out from one another, but both still seemed like viable options if no one better came along.

The last interview of the day pulled in and Emma read the name and her notes from his resume to refresh Cathy's memory.

"Sam Gray has about seven years' experience. He worked on the backside of the track for three years before switching to working with a hunter-jumper stable, and most recently, an eventing stable. Both were a similar size or slightly larger operation than ours. He made a note that the stable he works at now is being sold; they are downsizing and becoming a private farm due to the owner retiring, so he was no longer needed," Emma said.

"That does sound promising," Cathy added, smiling as the next interviewee slid out of his truck. Sam was tall with dark hair and tanned skin, probably from his long days working on farms. He wore a weathered ball cap and cowboy boots. He hadn't listed his age on the resume, but Emma guessed he was close to thirty.

As he reached them, he immediately offered his hand to Cathy and then to Emma, tipping his hat.

"Nice to make your acquaintance ma'ams," Sam said with a southern draw and a warm smile.

"Well, I don't normally like to be called ma'am since that makes me sound old," Cathy said smiling back, "but I suppose it doesn't make me sound quite so old when it's said in a southern accent," she added with a wink to Emma.

"I'm Emma, and this is Cathy," Emma said. Emma couldn't help but already like the warmth and kindness Sam seemed to radiate. Maybe it was a southern thing, but he just had a gentleness about him that he wore on his sleeve.

"I bet he's good with horses," she thought.

"Please, come have a seat," Cathy said, motioning towards their table. They sat across from Sam at the table, and Cathy scanned his resume once again.

"Well dear, you certainly have an impressive resume. And I see here your farm is downsizing; that is a shame," Cathy said. The way Cathy said it though, she didn't seem terribly disappointed. It was clear she already liked this young man. Their loss, our gain, Emma supposed.

"Yes, the Bennett's were wonderful to work for, but they simply don't want to run a large scale farm any longer since they are both in their seventies," Sam said, meeting Cathy's gaze with ocean blue eyes.

"Tell us a little more about your current position. What does a typical day look like?" Emma asked.

"I feed the horses, clean stalls, turnout, water, all the basics. I know how to tack up horses too, so if that's needed I can jump in and help with that as well," Sam said.

Emma and Cathy exchanged a quick glance of approval.

"And you would be comfortable with the fact that at this time we don't have a live in position available, correct?" Cathy asked.

"Yes ma'am, I have my own apartment anyway since the guys with more seniority at the farm I'm at occupy the living quarters," Sam replied.

"Perfect," Emma said, scratching notes down in her notebook.

"Do you mind terribly if I speak to Emma a moment in private?" Cathy asked, and Emma looked over at her curiously. They certainly had not planned this intermission, and she had not pulled her aside during any of the other interviews.

In front of the barn now, Cathy whispered to Emma.

"I think we should offer him this job on the spot. He is by far the most qualified candidate that's come through our doors today, and I feel like he would make an excellent addition to our team."

Emma had no reason to disagree with Cathy.

"Let's do it," Emma whispered back, smiling widely. Hiring their first candidate felt like such a strange, grown up, and exciting thing.

The two women walked back over and stood in front of the table. Sam stood up in response.

"Sam, we would like to officially offer you the position, if you're interested," Cathy said.

"Well, ma'am, I'll be honest. I really like everything about what y'all have going on here. After reading your help wanted posting, it seems like it would be a good fit as well. I don't reckon any other place I'll interview at will compare to this place, so yes, I would like to accept," Sam replied.

Cathy looked like she was ready to hug the young man but restrained herself, probably so she wouldn't scare him off if he wasn't one to be hugged by strangers. Emma was sure it was only a matter of time though.

"That's wonderful news!" Cathy said, beaming as she clasped her hands together in excitement, probably still keeping herself from hugging a perfect stranger.

"Welcome to the team," Emma said, smiling broadly at her soon-to-be coworker. She couldn't help but think he and Michael would get along. In a way, Sam reminded her a little bit of Michael.

They promised to be in touch about the details of his first day and waved as he drove off. Emma and Cathy chatted about their new hire, then Cathy excused herself to get something from her car, returning moments later with a bottle of champagne that had clearly been chilled in a cooler until now.

"I hoped we would have an excuse to pop this open," Cathy said, taking off the top, using the table in the barn as she poured them each a glass.

"Cheers to our first employee," Emma said, taking a sip.

"Second actually," Cathy said, raising her glass, her eyes sparkling with the same look as when she had told Emma of the other new employee. As if on cue, Emma heard the tires of a truck on the concrete outside the barn.

"Is that the other farm hand you hired?" Emma asked, as she set the glass back down on the table, ready to make her way outside to meet this new co-worker Cathy seemed so excited about.

"I think he will be perfect to help you keep the farm running smoothly," she added as she followed behind Emma as they made their way outside.

The truck in front of them was parked straight, and the glare of the sun made it impossible for her to get a sneak peek at the person sitting in the driver's seat.

But as soon as his boots hit the ground, she gasped audibly.

"Michael?" Emma said, jaw dropped.

"Sorry, Em, Cathy made me promise to keep it a secret until everything was official," Michael said, holding his hands in front of him defensively, but smiling playfully anyway. Emma spun around to where Cathy casually leaned against the barn door, smiling mischievously.

"You hired Michael?!" Emma asked, shock dripping from each word.

"Surprise," Cathy muttered, still grinning.

Emma whipped her head back to Michael and then to Cathy again, still reeling. Cathy hired Michael behind her back? Cathy was no stranger to her and Michael's deep friendship or the way he had done his best to protect her when Bo had been stalking her. Emma had also talked numerous times about how great Michael was to work with at Twin Oaks and how wonderful he was with the horses. So, in retrospect, it made complete sense why Cathy would jump through the hoops she surely had to get Michael to leave Twin Oaks and work for them.

Staring at Michael in front of her, standing on the very farm they would now *both* working at, her mind raced with a hundred different thoughts. Michael was her best friend, and she had missed working with him every day, that much was still true. But when he had kissed her, it had changed everything. More importantly, it had made leaving Twin Oaks feel like the best choice even if Cathy hadn't offered her this job, simply because of the guilt she felt about it. The last thing she wanted was to put additional strain on her relationship which had enough stress on it as it was.

Of course, Cathy didn't know about any of that. To Cathy, she had simply hired someone she and Emma both knew and trusted. Emma suddenly remembered this mysterious employee she had claimed to hire would be living onsite. That brought another mixed wave of emotions. On one hand, there was no one else in this world she trusted more than Michael to share this place she would now call home. On the other, she feared it would only magnify any feelings he may secretly have for her, if her theory about that was correct.

Emma wasn't sure how long she had been standing there staring at them as she processed this information, but the look on Cathy's face prompted her to finally say something else.

"That's great!" Emma said to Cathy, perhaps overdoing the enthusiasm. Once glance at Michael though, and she could tell he had seen right through her over-enthusiastic reaction.

"I couldn't help but make it a surprise, especially since I wasn't sure if I was going to be able to pull him away from Twin Oaks at first," Cathy added, winking at Michael.

"I'm actually surprised you left too," Emma said, turning back towards Michael.

"Cathy is very hard to say no to," he said with his typical low chuckle. "She finally wore me down with an offer I couldn't refuse," Michael said with a shrug.

Cathy *was* hard to say no to, that she knew firsthand.

"Well go on, show him his new apartment," Cathy said, shooing them toward the staircase at the end of the barn's exterior. Emma led the way up the stairs, opening the door to the barn apartment.

"This place is much nicer than the RV," Michael said as he opened the door to the bedroom, his eyes scanning the room.

"What are you going to do with the RV?" she asked curiously.

"Actually, it's not mine. I guess it kind of feels that way since I've lived there for so long. But it's owned by Twin Oaks," Michael replied.

Michael continued going through the apartment, looking pleased with his soon-to-be home. Suddenly, he turned back toward Emma, meeting her gaze and his expression softened. His voice was just as quiet as his expression as he spoke.

"It is ok I took this job, right?"

Emma blinked, staring back into his green eyes. If she wasn't sure before about him reading her face earlier when she found out about them being co-workers again, she was now. He truly seemed ready to walk away from this if she so much as said the word. It wasn't that she didn't want to work with him every day;

in fact, that was the problem. She wanted nothing more than to spend every day with him again. Just not at the expense of her relationship with Liam.

"What's left of it anyway," she thought.

"Of course I want you here," she said just as softly as he had spoken, touching his shoulder. "You are the only person I could ever trust to live on property with me, and to help me run this place. You are the person I rely on the most when things go south, like they always seem to," Emma exhaled, shaking her head. "I'm glad you're going to be part of this team Michael, truly."

She would just have to figure the rest out as they went. After all, Michael was a gentleman; feelings or not he wouldn't make the mistake of making any moves again while she was still with Liam.

"Ok, good. It's just the way you looked when you found out...," Michael said, trailing off.

Emma waved her hand, cutting him off. "I know. I panicked. It's just because of our history, but I'm glad it's you that got out of that truck today and not a stranger," Emma replied.

"Emma, I wouldn't do anything to ruin your relationship with Liam. You love him, I get it. That kiss was a mistake I told you that, remember? I won't let anything like that come between our friendship again," he promised.

Emma stared back at him, this time not sure how to respond. She shifted her weight uncomfortably, and Michael picked up on it immediately. "Sorry Em, I didn't mean to mention the kiss again...,"

"Actually, I haven't told Liam I love him," she blurted out. "He told me he loved me that weekend I went to Wellington, but I just couldn't say it back. Not when I don't know where we are headed. I mean we live in different cities for crying out loud!" Emma bit her lip, fighting back unexpected tears that suddenly welled behind her eyes.

"Emma, I had no idea. I thought everything was going well between the two of you," he said, placing his hand on her arm trying to comfort her without causing her to feel uncomfortable.

"I mean we are ok, I guess, but this long-distance thing and all the secrets...well they are eating me up inside," she stammered.

Michael didn't seem to know what to say, so he slid his hand down her arm, taking her hand instead. They met one another's gaze again, and Emma regretted not telling him what was really going on a long time ago. It felt good to talk about it with him and tell him the truth. After all, they didn't typically keep secrets from one another.

"If we are going to work together, and if I'm going to see you every day, I don't think I will be able to handle the guilt of keeping what happened between us a secret from Liam much longer," Emma admitted.

"That's your call Em. But it wasn't your fault, it was mine. You should not be carrying that guilt around," he said, his eyes reflecting how sorry he was for putting her in this position.

She knew that, of course. But still, she couldn't take feeling this way much longer.

"I don't know how he is going to react when I do finally tell him. I just hope he can forgive me for not telling him sooner," Emma said.

"He would be a fool not to. If he wants to be angry with someone, he can be angry with me," Michael said.

They were interrupted by the creak of the door as it swung open, and Cathy stepped into the room.

"Well, what do you think?" Cathy asked, completely unaware of what she had interrupted.

"What will Cathy think when she finds out?" Emma thought, feeling sick to her stomach at the thought of it. What would happen if Liam ended it with her after he found out? What would become of her and Cathy's relationship and the shared business? Cathy was like family now, a family she was tied to mainly because of her and Liam's relationship. If that went away, what would the consequences be?

"It's perfect, Cathy, thank you," Michael said, smiling genuinely at her.

"In that case, let's grab another glass of champagne and make a toast to our new Live Oaks team!" Cathy said, beaming again.

Cathy headed back down the stairs, and they followed behind.

Emma stopped short at the top of the stair landing, looking out across the farm from this bird's eye view.

She could only hope that things wouldn't be ruined before they even began.

Chapter Eight

The week before moving day, time passed in lurches.

One day would go by in the blink of an eye, and the next Emma felt like the day would never end. But finally, after so much stress and anticipation, the closing and moving day into Live Oaks Farm had come.

She had come to love the staff at Three Phases Farm, especially Don and Hank, and that made saying goodbye harder than she'd expected. Not seeing Lily everyday was something she still couldn't wrap her mind around either, but she was comforted to know she would be boarding Annie at Live Oaks in a couple months.

Of course, she would be seeing Ben David a little too since they still had not officially found a trainer. Emma still couldn't imagine being ready for such an important moment in her career without his training and guidance.

Cathy had been in a hurry to get off the phone with her and handle whatever last minute thing she was doing to prep the farm every time they had spoken this week. As predicted, she had hired a landscaper and had instructed Emma not to swing by the farm again until move in day. Cathy loved her surprises, and this was going to be no exception

As she packed up the last of her horse's things into her tack box, she couldn't help but feel a strong sense of deja vu. After all, they had moved barns three times in a little less than a year.

"But this is really the last time," she thought, closing the tack box.

Emma heard the familiar sound of the trailer's ramp hitting the ground outside and grabbed her tack to be loaded up. As soon as the trailer came into view, she smiled. The brand-new trailer had an icon of a large live oak with hanging Spanish moss next to the farm's name decaled on the side of the trailer.

Surely this was only the first of many things that Cathy had been doing behind the scenes this week.

Michael came out from around the other side of the trailer where she assumed he was opening the tack room door for her to load up their things.

They met one another's gaze and she smiled at him, letting the day's excitement get the best of her despite the reservations she still held about working together again. Emma had come to terms with the fact that they would just have to find their footing as both friends and coworkers again. They managed it for a short while at Twin Oaks, and she was determined to make it work at Live Oaks.

After loading up her horse and tack, Emma took one last look around her temporary home at Three Phases Farm. It seemed like only yesterday they arrived here, and here they were already moving on. She was sure the time she had stayed at the most impressive farm she had ever been to would stick with her for years to come.

As they pulled up to the gates of Live Oaks Farm, Emma scanned the freshly landscaped entrance. The flower beds were now mulched and filled with brightly colored tropical plants, and Cathy had added new bushes that lined the area between the flower beds and the fence line.

After punching in the gate code and leading the way for the truck and trailer behind her, she took in the rest of the freshly manicured grounds which looked even more stunning than they had before. The grass was perfectly cut, free of the sporadic twigs and weeds that once scattered the property. Glancing to her left, Emma saw the same assortment of tropical flowers and foliage was planted around the front of the house surrounding by stones. The landscapers had even dressed up the front of the barn area with potted plants.

"This place looks incredible," Emma said half under her breath as she got out of the car. Michael was also getting out of the truck and the look on his face gave away that he too was impressed by all Cathy's efforts of getting this place ready. Valentine let out a sharp, impatient whinny from the trailer, making it clear she was ready to check out her new home for herself. Emma and Michael both turned simultaneously towards the trailer, laughing at Valentine's side-eyed expression through the trailer window.

After her horse was settled into her new stall with a fresh flake of hay in front of her, Emma decided it was time to check out the house and see how crazy Cathy had gone getting it ready for her. Knowing Cathy, it was going to be above and beyond.

"Want to check out the house with me? It's sure to be over the top since Cathy had free rein setting it up," Emma asked.

"You let Cathy set up the *whole* thing?" Michael asked, eyes widening and clearly holding back a laugh.

"I know, I was supposed to pick out décor and bedding, but Cathy got sick of waiting and asked if it was ok to pick them out for me. It's probably going to be crazy elaborate, isn't it?" Emma replied with a slight sigh, shaking her head.

"Definitely," Michael said, already walking across the lawn towards the house. He was almost as eager as Emma was to see what Cathy had done with the place.

Opening the door, Michael let out a low, quick chuckle before throwing her an 'I told you so' look.

"This place looks like the cover of a magazine," she said, glancing around the open kitchen and living room area. Cathy had stuck with a modern farmhouse look with light neutral colors. She had purchased a light linen couch, dark wood farmhouse table with white table legs, and a matching TV stand.

Emma headed down the hall toward the bedrooms, first walking into her own room. A white comforter lay wrinkle free on a bed frame that matched the furniture in the living room and the dresser on the other side of the room.

Michael peeked his head in the bedroom as well, letting out another low chuckle as his eyes passed over the matching furniture.

"Did I just walk into a furniture store display?" he teased.

"Very funny Michael," she said, lightly punching his arm. "This place looks incredible, even if I will be living in a store display," she added with a teasing smile.

Of course, she had half expected this to be the result of letting Cathy takeover. Emma hadn't noticed before, since she had been distracted by the matching furniture, but there were a few pictures hanging on the bedroom walls. Emma walked up closer to the wood framed photographs, her eyes running over the images. The first was a picture Hailey had taken the day she bought Valentine after the trail ride. The second was a picture of Valentine grazing in the pasture that Emma had taken at Twin Oaks the first week she arrived in Florida. The last one at the far side of the room compelled Emma to lightly touch the image in front of her; it was a photograph of her first horse, Lexington, with a blue ribbon hanging from his bridle.

Emma suddenly remembered there being another, much larger picture in the living room but hadn't paid much attention to it since it was hard to make out based on where she was standing at the time. Walking down the hall and into the open living room, she saw the large picture that hung above the couch. She had never seen the picture before and wasn't even sure who took it, but her eyes were already welling with tears. In the picture she was looking into Valentine's eyes, with her hand resting on the mare's forelock. It was the kind of picture that seemed to really capture her connection with her mare.

Michael was leaning against the far wall, arms crossed with a devious look in his eyes, half smirking.

"Did you take this?" she asked but could already guess the answer was yes based on his expression.

"Guilty," he said, putting his hands in the air and smiling warmly.

"When did you take it?" she asked, turning back to stare at the picture again.

"It was maybe a few days after we got back to Ocala after being in Wellington. I walked out of the barn and saw you there, although you didn't see me," he said, shrugging casually. "It just looked like it was a moment worth capturing. I was going to show it to you later, but we got so busy preparing for the Million Dollar Grand Prix party and then after that…," he trailed off, clearly trying not to bring up the still sensitive subject.

"How did Cathy get it then?" she asked curiously.

"Well, Cathy told me she planned to stalk your social media and print some pictures she thought you would like to hang around the house. She asked if I had any ideas about which pictures, and when she did, I remembered taking this picture and sent it to her. I remembered you talking about your first horse too, so Cathy and I searched through your pictures and picked the other ones for your bedroom," he replied.

Emma blinked back tears, touched that they had both gone to all this trouble to make this place feel a little more like home for her. Without thinking, she spun around and threw her arms around Michael's neck. He seemed stunned at first, but slowly wrapped his arms around her back, pulling her into his chest. Standing there in his warm embrace, she couldn't help but feel thankful for him being the one who was on her team as she navigated managing this farm.

"Emma?"

The sound of the front door opening and Liam's voice echoed in the kitchen behind her. She automatically pulled back from Michael's arms, tossing him a brief awkward glance before she rounded the corner of the hallway.

"Hey!" she called back, her voice cracking slightly in surprise as she walked over to Liam. Kissing her on the cheek, he glanced around the living room taking in furniture and décor as well.

"Looks like Aunt Cathy really pulled out all her stops on this one, but I can't say I'm surprised," Liam said, laughing.

"She sure did, and she also framed some really sweet pictures of my horses too," Emma said, motioning towards the picture behind the wall.

Michael rounded the corner, hand extended, as he approached her and Liam.

"Hey man, how are you?" Michael asked as Liam shook his hand.

"Nice to see you, Michael. Congrats on the new position; I'm sure my aunt didn't take no for an answer?" Liam replied.

"She did not," Michael said with a laugh.

Emma fought the wave of nausea that flooded her as she watched them casually converse, like her secret might explode out of her at any moment. The saying 'secrets keep you sick' had never been truer. How could Michael seem so nonchalant around Liam?

"Breathe and keep your mouth shut; don't ruin this day for Cathy," she thought. Or herself, for that matter. Is a knock down drag out fight how she wanted to remember their first day at this farm? Certainly not.

Michael must have been thinking the same thing, not to mention he had promised not to do anything that would compromise her relationship with Liam again.

Liam walked further into the house, checking out the bedrooms and living room, making sly comments about the matching furniture like they had.

"Have you checked out the finished basement yet?" he called down the hallway as he approached the staircase leading to the lower level.

"That was the next place we were heading before you walked in," Emma said, feeling her cheeks flush slightly when she thought about the emotional embrace she had shared with Michael before he had walked in.

"Well, we may as well go see what elaborate set-up she made for herself down there," Liam said sarcastically as he headed down the stairs. Emma avoided looking over at Michael as she followed directly behind Liam with Michael a few feet behind her.

At the base of the stairs, the three of them stopped to take in the impressive room. The furniture downstairs had a remarkably similar look to the upstairs, and Emma could tell already from the open bedroom door this bedroom furniture matched hers. There was a full living room setup in the main part of the room.

What had them all staring though was the wall closest to the staircase, which had a picture of the back side of the property, displaying the rolling hills and live oak trees with the freshly risen sun shining behind it. It was a breathtaking photo, and Emma wondered when she had the picture taken and how on earth she managed to get a wall size image that quickly.

Liam chuckled lightly.

"See, I told you Aunt Cathy would pull out all the stops," he said, wrapping an arm around Emma's shoulders, pulling her closer. Emma felt a pang of discomfort at the public display of affection happening inches from where Michael stood.

"Should we go back up to the barn? I want to make sure everything is perfect for when the boarders arrive," Emma said, using it as an excuse to gently slip out of Liam's embrace. Plus, she really did want to throw some flakes of hay in the stalls and make sure everything was ready when the others arrived. Emma felt an intense sense of responsibility to make sure everything at this farm ran smoothly. After all, that was her job now, and the horses' care was her ultimate priority.

"Sure, Aunt Cathy should be pulling in any second anyway," Liam replied.

Emma remembered Liam telling her they were driving separately from Wellington since Cathy wanted to stay in Ocala a little while longer than he could. Once again, he was only here for a few days since he had responsibilities at work first thing Monday morning.

They exited out the lower-level door, and Emma beelined for the hay room. She tossed hay into the stalls where the incoming horses would be, then swept the aisle.

She could hear Liam and Michael just outside the open barn doors talking about a sports game they had both watched earlier that week. Emma tried to ignore it and focused on organizing the feed room instead.

A little while later she heard Cathy's car's tires hit the pavement and the metal gate closing behind her. Emma peeked her head out of the feed room door as she rounded the corner, seeing Liam hugging his aunt and Michael shaking her hand as they gushed about how great everything looked.

"Emma!" Cathy said cheerfully when Emma emerged from the barn.

"Cathy, this place looks perfect! You certainly worked your magic on it. And that house!" Emma shook her head, almost choking up as she recalled the gorgeous furniture and pictures of her horses.

"I'm glad you liked it, dear," Cathy said, rubbing her shoulder affectionately and meeting her gaze.

"I've got almost everything set up in the barn, other than what the boarders will be bringing with them," Emma said.

As if on cue, she could hear the rumbling of the truck and trailer coming down the back road and approaching the entrance.

They all turned to watch the hauler pull through the gates, and the horses whinnied from inside.

One by one, the team led all six horses off the trailer and put them in each of the prepared stalls. After the hauler was paid and on his way out, Cathy walked back into the barn where Emma, Liam, and Michael were finishing putting all the horses' tack and tack boxes away. All the horses had name tags on their halters so they were identifiable, but Emma was curious about the story behind each horse.

Cathy was running her hand up the forelock of a dark bay, a broad smile on her face when Emma emerged from the tack room after the last of the tack was put away.

"Who's this?" Emma asked softly, approaching Cathy and the dark bay.

"This is Cujo. Frankie, a good friend of mine from my days as a competitor, owns him. He competed him through advanced level, but since he's getting older one of his working students, Clara, is now competing him and is about to step up to the preliminary level. I'm sure you will meet her soon, and she is around your age too, I believe," Cathy said.

"I wouldn't mind having someone my age around the barn," she thought.

Cathy gave Cujo one last pat before continuing down the aisle, pausing briefly at the next stall over. "This is Arwen, a Warmblood. She started as a show jumper, but her amateur owner just bought her and started eventing her at novice level," she said, pointing at the gray mare. "That's Piper," Cathy said, pointing across the aisle at a chestnut mare. "Piper is an off-the-track Thoroughbred that just moved up to training level with her owner."

Cathy walked further down the barn aisle stopping at the next stall. "This is Moose, he's a Warmblood as well and his owner mostly competes in equitation and show jumpers, not eventing, but we didn't hold that against her since she is an old friend of mine," Cathy said with a wink.

"Over here is Buzz; he is still pretty green and just completed his first season at the beginner novice level. He is also an off-the-track Thoroughbred," Cathy said, patting the dapple grey gelding.

Cathy walked over to the last stall that housed a chestnut gelding, who didn't look up at the two women because he was far too busy taking in mouthfuls of hay.

"And finally, this is Manny. He actually just retired. He competed through advanced level with his owner who wanted him to have a safe place to call home in his golden years. Unfortunately, he didn't have the room to keep him at his farm and needed the stall for his horses in training."

Emma felt her heart swell as her eyes glanced around at the horses in the barn casually munching hay. It was a different feeling then when she had been in charge of the horses at Twin Oaks. She was both excited and nervous to be the person entrusted with their well-being.

"Have you moved your things from your apartment yet?" Cathy asked.

"No, not yet. I wanted to be sure the horses were settled in before I moved into the house. It's not like I have much to move anyway," Emma said with a half shrug.

"Liam, dear, why don't you take Emma back to her apartment and help her move her things? It will be dark before we know it," Cathy called down the aisle to her nephew.

Emma turned her head toward the feed room door and began opening her mouth to protest. The horses still needed grain, and she still felt like she had so much organizing to do in the feed room now that the boarding horses' supplements and food had arrived.

"Now, before you give me an excuse about the horses being fed, I'll have you know I am perfectly capable of feeding a handful of horses," Cathy said, anticipating her words and cutting Emma off before she had a chance to protest.

The respective owners *had* sent along paperwork with the feeding instructions for each horse, so really there was no reason to argue with Cathy. Not that Cathy was one to be argued with anyway.

"Well, ok, I guess it would be nice to get my things moved while it's still daylight," Emma said, reluctance still lingering in her voice.

"See you in a bit!" Cathy said, all but shooing Liam and Emma out the barn doors and toward Liam's car.

———*ele*———

Emma's eyes flew open fifteen minutes before her alarm went off. She sat up in her new bed, taking in the surroundings of her new room. Emma smiled when she caught a glimpse of the pictures of Valentine and Lexington on the wall in front of her.

It did not surprise her that her body was trying to pull her from slumber early. The subconscious excitement of waking up at her new home surely was responsible. However, she also realized there was a delicious smell wafting down the hallway that may have had something to do with it as well.

Emma rolled out of bed, sniffed the air and identified the smell as coffee mixed with breakfast foods.

"Mmm, Cathy must be cooking," she thought, her mouth already watering and stomach growling.

They had ordered a pizza late last night after she had finished moving her things into the house, but she had been so tired at that point that she didn't eat much before going to bed.

Now, Emma was ravenous.

They still had not had a chance to grocery shop, so Emma wondered if Cathy had done so this morning. Although, the nearest grocery store was still almost fifteen minutes away and it was barely dawn.

Emma tied her robe around her waist and walked down the hallway to the kitchen where Cathy was stirring scrambled eggs around a skillet.

"Good morning, Cathy! Where did all this come from?" Emma asked, her eyes scanning the array of breakfast foods being prepared.

"Good morning, my dear. I hope you are hungry! Oh, I just ran down the road last night after you went to bed to get a few things. There is fresh coffee in the pot and orange juice in the fridge," Cathy replied.

'A few things' was an understatement. Emma opened the fridge door to find it fully stocked.

"Cathy, you are a lifesaver, thank you," she said, relieved she didn't have to add grocery shopping to her list of things to do today.

"After you feed the horses, do you mind letting Michael know there is breakfast in here for him too? Liam is asleep downstairs still, but I can wake him up," Cathy said.

"Of course, I'm sure Michael will be thrilled. I doubt he has anything in his fridge yet either," Emma replied.

Emma changed quickly, and then slid on her rubber boots and headed out into the foggy morning. She breathed deeply, enjoying that fresh morning air that seemed to have just a little extra salt and moisture to it. The sun was just beginning to rise, and her assumptions about how stunning the sunrise would look behind this farm did not disappoint.

The horses called out low nickers as she slid the barn door open, and she smiled when she saw seven horse heads hanging out of their stall doors, ears pricked in her direction. While her apartment had been nice, and Ben David's farm had been an incredible experience, she almost forgot how much she missed waking up on the farm and being the first person to walk through those barn doors for the day.

It was funny how her perspective about what she wanted for her future had shifted a little too. When she considered leaving Twin Oaks, prior to Cathy's offer to run her farm, she imagined herself at a mega farm similar to Ben's. However, now that she had experienced both, she realized how much she enjoyed running a smaller scale farm with just herself and a few staff members. There was something magical about being so intimately involved with each and every horse's day so completely.

Horses continued to call out as she prepared the feed buckets, adding the appropriate supplements to each. Emma always found it funny how different each horse's personality was at feeding time.

Manny stood like a perfect gentleman, only letting out a low nicker now and then before she poured his feed into a rubber ground feeder, sliding it under the door as he casually lipped at it.

Arwen tossed her head up and down, making low nicker sounds until her food was within reach. Piper paced her stall, making little crop circles in her bedding until her food was in her feed bucket. Moose pawed the ground, exposing the rubber mat under his bedding until he was fed. Buzz called out non-stop, but still remained fairly still with his head hanging out, and Cujo had joined Buzz in a back-and-forth call, as if to remind Emma not to forgot them. Valentine had always been fairly polite at breakfast time, although she was letting out a few extra nickers today no thanks to the encouragement from her new neighbors, Cujo and Buzz.

Emma threw flakes of hay to the horses that were now quiet except for the sound of crunching grain. She leaned against the wood wall, watching them eat for a moment, smiling.

Hearing the creak of the wooden stairs, she turned her head to see Michael coming through the barn doors at the other end of the aisle.

"Good morning, co-worker," Emma said warmly. "Cathy has made up an impressive breakfast spread and invited you up to eat with us."

"Great, I was planning to eat a protein bar since that's all I have, but that sounds *way* better," Michael replied, his warm smile peeking out from under his ball cap-covered face. It was strange and familiar at the same time to see Michael first thing in the barn like this again. They may be at a different farm now, but she couldn't help feeling a sense of comfort having him here helping her run the place, despite the circumstances of their past.

"Did you sleep ok in your new apartment? Did the horses keep you up? I know you're used to being in an RV across the property," Emma asked.

"Nah, they didn't keep me up. They aren't very loud at night anyway. If anything, I kind of like being able to hear them now and then and know everything is ok down here," Michael replied.

"I'm glad. I think I'll sleep better at night knowing you're here too," Emma replied, her eyes meeting his.

As soon as she said it, she worried about how he would perceive her words. Of course, she was referring to the horses, but if she was honest with herself, she was referring to her own feeling of safety as much as the horses. Emma had imagined what life would be like at a farm by herself if they purchased one with no other living quarters on property. Or, what it would be like if a stranger had moved into the barn apartment on this property before she knew it was Michael who had been hired? Neither option made her feel entirely safe, but maybe that as a little PTSD from her stalker incident. The moment she learned it was Michael, her subconscious relaxed just knowing he would be here if things hit the fan, regardless of the tension between them because of the kiss.

"I'm glad you feel that way," he said, still holding her gaze.

The vague answer and no readable facial expression didn't indicate how he had taken it, but she wasn't about to go into that complex issue by taking the conversation any deeper.

"Ready to head up to the house?" Emma asked, changing the subject and dropping her gaze.

"Definitely," Michael said, leading the way back out the barn doors toward the house.

Sam Gray, their new farm hand, would be here in a little less than an hour giving them just enough time to eat before needing to show him around.

Cathy had clearly been hard at work while Emma had been in the barn, because now she had also made waffles and pancakes in addition to the other breakfast food she had prepared before Emma left the house.

Liam was sitting at the table already, sipping coffee with his laptop open in front of him, probably checking work emails if Emma had to guess.

"Good morning," Emma said, walking over to Liam who stood up and planted a kiss on her cheek before returning to his work.

"Mornin' man," Michael said politely to Liam, who responded with a "good morning" as well. It still rattled her emotions and anxiety when the two of them were in the same room, and she hoped she could keep it together when they all sat down for breakfast.

Emma sometimes wished she wasn't so convicted about lying, even though deep down she knew it was a respectable quality to have. In this instance though, it was only wreaking havoc on her mental health.

Cathy took over the conversation, giving Emma a reason to say less and eat more. She had never been more thankful for Cathy's talkative nature. The conversation was mainly directed at Michael since Cathy knew the least about him and was not one to keep endless questions to herself when she was getting to know someone better. Emma recalled meeting Cathy for the first time; it had been a similar scenario.

Emma checked her watch, sensing it was getting close to the time Sam would be arriving.

"We had better head to the barn; Sam will be here any minute," she said, looking at Michael. Michael stood up and tipped his hat respectfully as he thanked Cathy for breakfast.

"I will be right behind you dears. I just need to freshen up," Cathy replied, heading to the stairwell that led to the finished basement.

"I feel like I was just re-interviewed," Michael said, laughing a little as he spoke.

"Don't worry, that's just Cathy. If it makes you feel better, I know she likes you, which is probably why she wants to know every single thing about you," Emma replied, giving him a playful shove as they walked towards the barn.

Emma began sweeping the aisle, and Michael began fixing the latch on an empty stall that was broken prior to moving in. It was almost like being back at Twin Oaks for a moment, and even day one at this farm they found their rhythm of working together easily like they had before.

They both looked up from their work simultaneously when they heard a truck door shut. Sam's tall frame came into view as he headed toward the open barn doors where Emma and Michael now stood.

"You must be Sam; it's nice to meet you man," Michael said, offering his hand which Sam shook enthusiastically, flashing them broad smile.

"Nice to see you again, Miss Emma," Sam said politely in his southern draw, shaking her hand again.

"You as well," Emma replied, returning his smile with one of her own. With all the other excitement of preparing to move, she had almost forgotten how much she liked Sam. He was undoubtedly going to make an excellent member of their team.

Emma and Michael led the way further into the barn as they showed Sam around the feed and tack rooms, introducing him to the horses along the way. He ran his hand gently up Cujo's forelock, and Emma was sure in that moment they had chosen the right person for the job. His gentle nature toward the horses immediately made Emma feel like she could trust him, even if she wasn't around. Emma explained that she would be feeding the horses in the morning and Sam could plan to start cleaning stalls when he arrived in the morning first thing, and he could throw feed in the evening.

They headed out back, showing him the rest of the property. They now stood in the back field, where they had been going over the different pastures, discussing which horses would be turned out together and where.

"Is this where you will be putting up the cross country course?" Sam asked, pointing at the open, unfenced field with a couple scattered trees that sat on the back side of the property.

"It is, and actually Cathy has the cross country jumps arriving tomorrow, and then the farm updates will be complete in time for Saturday. By the way, we are hosting a grand opening party here that day, and Cathy will never forgive me if I didn't invite you. It will be one of those come and go as you please type parties, and it runs between 4:00 pm and 8:00 pm," Emma replied.

Emma was thankful for Sam's question for she was sure she would have forgotten to invite him.

"Cathy goes all out for her parties, so bring your appetite," Michael added, chuckling a little as he spoke.

"That sounds like a great time; I will be sure to stop by. Please tell Miss Cathy thank you for the invitation," Sam replied.

"You are very welcome!" Cathy's voice called out from a little ways behind them. Emma, Michael, and Sam turned around simultaneously to see Cathy striding across the grass toward them.

"Sam, it's nice to see you again. Welcome officially to the Live Oaks team," Cathy said enthusiastically.

Sam nodded, shaking her hand. They all turned back around toward the gorgeous view of the back half of the farm that lay in front of them.

"This farm is beautiful," Sam added, his eyes still locked on the slow rolling, oak tree-dotted hills.

"It really is," Emma added, almost breathlessly.

Truly, she wasn't sure how she had managed to get so lucky, despite the circumstances that brought her here.

Eventually, they peeled themselves away from the horizon and headed back to the barn. Sam, who Emma was quickly realizing was a self-starter, grabbed a wheelbarrow and began picking stalls. Michael headed out to the fence line where he had spotted a loose board on the walk back, and Emma pulled Cujo out of his stall.

Clara had called Emma late yesterday asking if she could lunge him for her since Clara was held up at her farm working late. She had said he was quite the pistol when he wasn't worked consistently. Cujo's personality reminded her so much of Jimmie John, and she happily agreed to work him for her. After all, it was part of her job and a service the farm offered the boarders, not that she minded one bit.

Clipping the lunge line to Cujo's halter, she clucked to him as she sent him out. Cujo's trot was big, and he shook his head, threatening to break into a canter after only a couple trot steps. Emma smiled. She couldn't help but love his spicy personality. She had always been drawn to this type of horse for some subconscious reason. Emma was fairly certain Clara would be someone she got along with, especially since they both were, or had been, working students and clearly had a similar taste in horses. Cujo cantered around in a circle in front of her, offering a buck now and then before bolting briefly. Emma laughed at his enthusiasm, now even more curious about what the horse was like under saddle.

Emma gave the now sweaty Cujo a cold hose bath and proceeded to pull out a few of the other horses that owners had requested to be worked. It felt nice to be past the pressures and anxiety that she felt in her limbo period before they purchased the farm. She enjoyed it being just her and the horses right now, even if she knew they would eventually have a trainer here half the day in the near future.

They had not yet found the perfect trainer for Live Oaks Farm, so for now, working the client horses to the best of her abilities was her responsibility. Although, when they did have the additional help of a trainer, she couldn't say she wasn't excited to go young horse shopping with Cathy.

Not that she couldn't handle a young, green horse. Emma had ridden them on a regular basis back home in Ohio and at Twin Oaks. But once those horses were ready to move up the levels past her comfort zone, a professional trainer was certainly needed. In order for these young prospect horses to be sold at the amount they needed for the farm to profit, they needed the experience and training a professional could give them.

Maybe someday, and certainly this was Emma's goal, she could be both the trainer and barn manager for Live Oaks Farm as well. But getting more comfortable with the other phases in eventing she was still fairly new to, and at the higher levels after that, was step one.

For now, she was happy to be in charge of this farm and riding the horses up to the levels to which she was comfortable.

Emma turned the hose off, and ran the squeegee over Piper's back, flinging excess water off her gleaming wet coat. Piper was her last horse that needed worked for the day, and as she led her down the aisle back to her stall, Emma could hear Michael on the riding lawn mower across the property and Sam in the feed room prepping the grain for evening feed.

Emma leaned against Valentine's stall, and her head was already hanging out, ears pricked in the direction of the feed room. Putting one hand under her mare's chin, she stroked her velvety fur as she took in the moment.

It was almost like an, "I made it," moment for Emma. Here she was managing her own farm, living in a gorgeous house, and making a living doing what she loved with the best staff she could have asked for.

Emma closed her eyes a moment, living in the perfection of this day.

She hoped this was only the beginning of a magical horse-filled future for her.

Chapter Nine

Emma had been warned; summers in Florida were brutal.

Each day it was as if someone was turning up the dial on temperature and humidity just a little bit higher.

Now, the air was so thick and hot she could hardly breathe if it was after 11:30 am. Still, she would take this hot sticky mess of a climate over the long, brutally cold winters of Ohio.

At least, that's what she was telling herself as sweat ran down her forehead onto her brow, threatening to roll into her eyes for the second time in the last hour. She quickly wiped it away before continuing her work.

Cathy, bless her heart, was frantically doing what she could to help perfect this farm before tonight's grand opening party. Although, so far, that had only consisted of making a long list of tasks for each of them. Emma couldn't say she was surprised; she knew how important this event was to Cathy. Parties were Cathy's thing anyway.

Combining her intense regular party planning with a farm's (specifically the first farm Cathy had ever owned) grand opening was a recipe for a very long, intense day for all of them.

Emma could hear the sound of the weedwhacker in the distance. Cathy had tasked poor Michael with weed-whacking every inch of this place, including around the new cross country jumps in the back field that had been delivered recently. Needless to say, Michael would be getting his steps in today. Emma made a mental note to run to the house and put on a pot of coffee when they were done getting things ready if they were going to survive the four-hour party later in the day.

The faint sound of Cathy's voice in the distance and the squeak of the metal joints on the party tables Sam had been assigned to set up could also be heard in the front part of the property. Emma had been cleaning every inch of the barn since she finished feeding and cleaning stalls this morning. Sam had been stolen away by Cathy an hour ago, leaving Emma to finish the last half of the stalls he hadn't had a chance to complete.

Emma liked to keep a clean barn anyway, but this place probably hadn't looked *this* clean since the day it was built. Wiping away yet another trickle of sweat from just above her eye, she set down the rag she had been using to wipe down the stall fronts. Standing up, she headed down the aisle towards the staircase leading to Michael's barn apartment. The house was so much further away than Michael's conveniently located apartment, and her water bottle had been empty for far too long.

If there was one thing she had learned living in Florida, it was to stay hydrated, especially on a hot day like today. Michael had mentioned that if she ever needed to grab something to drink that she was more than welcome to raid his fridge, and today seemed like the perfect opportunity to take him up on his offer. Until today, she hadn't really needed to. Normally Emma would refill her water bottle at her own fridge in the house while taking a quick break in the air conditioning.

Today, however, was not that kind of day. Because Cathy was in full party planning mode, there was going to be barely enough time to get everything as perfect as Cathy wanted in time for the party. Not to mention she would need to take time to shower and get herself presentable.

Emma opened the door to Michael's place and was surprised how clean it was. Not that she expected him to be messy per se, but most of the guys she had dated in the past weren't exactly neat. He had several pairs of cowboy boots lined up on a rug by the front door, a jacket hung on a hook on the wall, a dish in the sink from breakfast, but otherwise, it was tidy.

Pulling open the refrigerator door, Emma pulled out a bottle of water and chugged the entire thing as she stood with the fridge door agape, letting the cold air wash over her. Pulling out another water bottle to take with her, she shut the fridge door and gave the room a quick scan as she headed for the staircase.

A framed picture on the corner of the TV stand caught her eye. Truth be told, she hadn't planned on being nosy, even if this was the first time she had been in his apartment since he moved in.

Without thinking, she strode across the room towards the picture. She gently picked it up and looked at the image of a young woman with dark brown hair sitting in a chair by a lake. The photo had caught her mid-laugh, her face happy and glowing.

It didn't take much for Emma to assume that this must be Jane, Michael's fiancé who had passed away.

"She's gorgeous," Emma thought.

Emma continued to stare at the twenty-something year old girl gone too soon from this world. A woman Michael had wanted to be his wife, and clearly still held feelings for since he kept her picture in his living room. How could he not? She was beautiful and kind, from she knew about her.

She wasn't sure why him having a picture of his late fiancé had tugged at a nerve. They were only friends, and she had a boyfriend, after all. Still, her deep suspicions of his feelings for her felt somehow shallow knowing he kept Jane's picture displayed like this.

Emma set the picture where she found it before heading back down to the barn. She had a lot of work to do, and she didn't have time to be mulling over Michael's private life.

When Emma made her way back down to the barn, a young woman who appeared to be around her age was at Cujo's stall, scratching his neck. Cujo's head was cocked, and he was leaning into her hand clearly enjoying the affection.

"You must be Clara!" Emma said enthusiastically as she walked towards the slender woman with light brown hair.

"And you must be Emma," Clara replied, smiling widely at her.

"It's so nice to finally meet you," Emma added.

"Thanks for taking such good care of Cujo; he seems very happy here," Clara said, shooting a glance and the dark bay whose ears were pricked in their direction. "I hope you don't mind, I see you all are trying to get things ready for the party later, but I was hoping to take Cujo on a gallop out back and maybe take a few cross country fences?"

"Of course! I'm not going to lie, I'm jealous you get to test it out. We have been so busy getting things ready for this grand opening that I haven't had time to take my horse back there yet and jump around," Emma replied.

"Well, when you aren't so busy, we should definitely plan a day to ride together. It's only fun riding alone so many times, you know?" Clara said.

"I would love that," Emma replied, smiling warmly at her.

"I'll see you around then," Clara said as she slid the halter over Cujo's ears, leading him out of the stall towards the grooming bay.

"See you!" Emma replied, heading to where she had set the rag down fifteen minutes ago now.

Emma stuck the now dry rag in the bucket of soapy water as she began wiping down the second to last stall in the barn.

Still, for some reason, she couldn't get the picture of Jane from her mind.

ele

Emma shot a glance at the clock on her nightstand as she placed one last bobby pin in her half up hair style.

"3:58...shoot!" She thought, all but jogging to the sun dress she had laid out for tonight's grand opening party. Cathy would have her head if she was late for their own party. Plus, Michael would surely tease her for not being on time for an event, as usual.

To be fair, she had been helping Cathy with last minute decorations until the last possible minute. She had barely had enough time to shower and dry her hair when it was all said and done. Let alone the power nap she had hoped to take before this party.

Emma pulled the dark navy, mid-length dress over her hourglass frame and slipped into the sandals she had picked out to go with it. She had considered wedge heels, but after being on her feet all day today, Emma had firmly decided against them and pulled these out before her shower.

A light knock at her door pulled her from her thoughts.

"Coming!" she said, as she spun around and headed to her bedroom door.

"Hey, it's me," Liam's voice said as he cracked the door open, quickly looking Emma up and down, his eyes passing over the flattering dress she was wearing.

"You look amazing, as always," he said in his typical smooth, charming voice, giving her quick kiss. "But Aunt Cathy will hunt us both down in," he glanced at his watch, "thirty seconds if we don't get out there."

"She sure will. Let's go," Emma replied, following him down the hall in a hurry.

As they walked out the front door of the house, Emma saw there was already a handful of guests mingling around the bar where the hired bartender was pouring a glass of wine for one of them. A long table with two caterers ran the length of one side of the barn, and string lights that Cathy had the guys hang from the roof to some of the trees twinkled above them. Emma had wondered why they were necessary, since the sun wouldn't start setting until late in the party, but she knew talking Cathy out of something like that was a battle she would never win.

"Em!" she heard a familiar voice say somewhere behind a group of people.

"Lily!" Emma replied, wrapping her friend up in a hug when she reached her. It was so nice having the support of her friend here. She already missed seeing her on a daily basis.

"I'm going to say hi to some of my aunt's friends, Em. I'll let you two catch up," Liam said, excusing himself as he headed toward Cathy.

"I see Cathy outdid herself, as usual," Lily said with a laugh as she looked around at the lavish decor.

"You know it," Emma replied, shaking her head and laughing a little as well. "Hey, there is someone I want you to meet," Emma added. She led her over to Clara, who was chatting with one of the other boarders.

"Lily, this is Clara. She rides Cujo, one of the boarded horses here. Clara, this is my good friend, Lily. She will be boarding her horse here as well when she starts vet school in the fall," Emma said.

"It's so nice to meet you, Lily. I was just telling Emma this morning that I would love to plan riding time together. You should definitely join us once you bring your horse over here!" Clara said.

"We could be like the adult eventing saddle club!" Lily replied.

All three women laughed at the mental image. Still, Emma couldn't help but enjoy the thought of having other young women to ride with. It was one thing she missed most about Maggie's barn back home; that horse riding comradery Hailey, Lily, and the other girls shared there was priceless.

Emma saw Michael and Sam making their way towards her.

"Hey guys, perfect timing! Sam, this is my good friend, Lily, and one of our boarders, Clara," Emma said, pointing them out as she spoke.

Sam nodded and tipped his hat to Lily before offering her his hand. "Ma'am," he said politely, a twinkle in his eye. Sam offered his hand to Clara as well, apologizing for being busy that morning and not having a chance to introduce himself earlier. Emma couldn't be sure, but the way Sam looked at Lily made her smirk a little.

"It's a shame she is still seeing that other guy. Those two would be perfect for each other," she thought.

"Clara, it's nice to meet you. Nice seeing you again, Lily. Are you excited to start vet school in a couple months?" Michael asked.

Almost thirty minutes passed in a blur as the five of them stood laughing, talking, and getting to know each other.

Emma quickly excused herself from the group, knowing she really needed to mingle with the other guests now that most of them had arrived. The DJ must have been setting up while she was deep in conversation because all of a sudden music filled the air. She made her way through the crowd, talking to riders, trainers, and horse owner friends of Cathy's, graciously accepting their congratulations on the opening of their new farm.

It almost felt like a dream; one she could have hardly imagined possible a little less than a year ago. Emma weaved her way through the small crowd, past where some had made their way to the grassy makeshift dancefloor as she finally reached Cathy and Liam.

"Well Cathy, I think it's safe to say this party is a success!" she said, smiling towards the proud farm owner who hadn't wiped a smile off her face all night.

"You very well might be right, my dear," Cathy replied, her eyes sweeping over the clusters of horse professionals and friends, some of which Emma had learned she had known for nearly twenty years.

"Thank you for all your help bringing everything together today, and please let Michael and Sam know how much I appreciate their hard work as well," Cathy said.

"Of course, I will be sure to pass that along," Emma replied.

"Why don't you and Liam go take a spin on the dance floor? You've done your mingling; go have a good time!" Cathy said, all but pushing them out into the small group of couples who were dancing close to a slow, country song.

Liam took Emma's hand as he led her to the dance floor. Emma rested her hand on his shoulder as he swept one arm around her waist, and they swayed back and forth slowly to the beat of the song.

Liam held her gaze, and Emma couldn't help but wonder when they would be together next now that the excitement of moving and opening the farm was over.

"Sorry we haven't had much of a chance to spend time together lately," Liam said, reading her face like a book. "I just keep hoping work will slow down but…," he trailed off.

"I know," Emma replied, her voice cracked and short.

"But it's not going to," Emma thought. This felt like deja vu. How many times had they had this conversation? On top of that, the guilt about what happened between her and Michael felt like an invisible wall that had been between them for months now. A wall he knew nothing about.

They danced on, saying nothing else for the first half of the next song. Glancing at Liam now and then, she felt the words bubbling up a little more as each second ticked by.

Emma knew this time bomb had been ticking for far too long. It was the kind of word bomb that would free her guilty conscious but destroy everything in its path in the same instance.

"Not tonight," she thought. Cathy's party was nothing short of perfection. The song was almost over now.

"I can't do this to Cathy. Not tonight…," she thought again, trying to reason with herself. But the words were all but caught in her throat now, threatening to come out if she so much as opened her mouth.

Her body tensed, and she willed it to relax.

"Em, you ok?" Liam asked, one eyebrow raised quizzically as he scanned her face.

Too late.

"Secrets keep you sick," she thought, remembering the phrase that seemed to keep coming to mind.

Emma shook her head side to side, tears welling up now. Refusing to speak, she knew the words would certainly tumble out right here in the middle of the dance floor in front of everyone.

Emma grabbed Liam's hand and pulled him silently towards the barn doors, shutting them behind her quickly.

The dam that held her tongue before broke the moment the barn doors latched shut.

"Michael kissed me," Emma blurted out.

"Why did I say it like that?" she thought, instant guilt of how she had presented this information now replacing the original guilt she felt keeping the secret.

Exactly ten seconds passed between the time she spoke the words aloud and the time Liam muttered a breathless, "What?"

Ten seconds that felt like one hundred.

He was staring wide-eyed at her, his jaw hung loosely. He didn't mutter another word. He just kept staring at her with a look of shock and hurt that she knew would haunt her later.

"It was the night of the Million Dollar Grand Prix Party at Twin Oaks. We both had a lot to drink, not that it's any excuse, but Michael walked me to my guesthouse and he just...," Emma trailed off.

She couldn't say the words out loud a second time.

"He felt horrible about it the second it happened. He told me to forget it ever happened, and well, we did. We are just friends. We always have been but...," she trailed off again, her throat felt swollen and hoarse all of a sudden.

Liam still stared at her, absorbing the information as she rambled on.

"I'm so sorry, Liam. I wanted to tell you before but I just...I couldn't...," her voice broke halfway through the last word. What else could she say at this point?

The wave of relief for getting this lie off her chest felt hollow. The betrayal in Liam's eyes said what he hadn't yet. She had crushed him.

Liam said nothing but spun around and flung open the barn doors. Emma's heart sank and she felt the blood drain from her face.

This was it; the perfect party was about to be ruined. And it was all her fault.

Liam marched directly towards the unsuspecting Michael, who was casually chatting with Sam at the other end of the party.

Michael looked up seconds before Liam's hands made contact with his chest, shoving him backwards with a force that made Emma gasp as she watched the events unfolding before her.

"This is all my fault...," Emma murmured almost silently under her breath.

Michael stumbled back, a stunned look on his face at first. But the realization of Liam's aggressive display crossed his face quickly, replacing shock with remorse.

"Listen, I'm so sorry man. I know I shouldn't have...," Michael began, his words interrupted by Liam shoving Michael backwards a second time. This time Michael didn't catch himself and fell into the fence behind him.

A cracking sound ripped through the now quiet farm as his back split the board it landed on.

"LIAM!" An exasperated Cathy could be heard reprimanding him, shock in her own voice at his seemingly random act of aggression toward Michael.

At the sound of his aunt's voice, Liam froze, his fists clenched, and his face filled with a mixture of anger and hurt as he turned around to meet her gaze.

"I'm so sorry, Aunt Cathy," Liam said shortly. He spun on his heels, walking quickly toward his car parked near the house. Emma had tears pouring down her face now as she jogged after Liam, feeling the eyes of every person there shift from Liam to her.

"Liam!" she called out to him as he was opening his car door. He paused, turning toward her but said nothing.

"I'm so sorry. I promise, nothing has happened since and we are just friends...," she added, before Liam held up his hand, cutting her off.

"How could you lie to me about it, all this time? Let me hold conversations with the guy who kissed *my* girlfriend like nothing happened?" Liam asked, his voice filled with emotion.

"I'm so sorry Liam," she said weakly, unsure what else to add.

"Emma, I care for you, you know I do but...," Liam shook his head, closing his eyes a moment before he spoke again. "I think we need to take some time apart. I think we should take a break."

"A break?" she croaked.

"What does that even mean?" she thought.

Before Emma had time to ask any further questions, he quickly kissed her on the cheek, meeting her gaze for half a second with a somber look before sliding quickly into the driver's seat of his car, shutting it as he simultaneously hit the gas pedal towards the front gate.

Emma stood there unmoving, watching him tear down the driveway and onto the back road until he was out of sight.

The thing about reality is that it has a way of lulling you into a false sense of security. One minute all is right in the world, as if bad things simply happen to other people. But they happen to everyone.

And they seem to happen just when things couldn't be going better.

Chapter Ten

Emma opened her eyes, wishing she could simply roll over and go back to sleep. At least when she was asleep, she didn't have to deal with the reality of everything that had happened last night.

After Liam had left in a whirlwind, Emma had stood there far too long, letting tears fall and guilt rip through her. Sure, *she* hadn't kissed Michael, but she had kept it a secret for far, far too long, destroying Liam in the process. And for that, she might also never forgive herself for ruining a very special night for someone to whom she owed everything.

"Cathy," she whispered aloud. What was she going to tell Cathy? Or had Liam already spilled the beans about the entire thing? If he had, what would Cathy think of her now?

For all she knew, her job could be on the chopping block for what she did. Emma had considered that once the secret was out that the repercussions of it would cause more than a little tension between her and Cathy. After all, Liam was practically her son. And she was no one to her without a relationship to Liam.

Sure, Cathy had said that the fact she was dating her nephew had little impact on her decision to hire her as Live Oaks Farm's barn manager, but that was before this messy break-up. Er, break. Emma still wasn't even sure exactly what that meant. Were they technically still together?

Emma shut her eyes again, feeling the tension headache that was already forming near her eyes make its way back to the rest of her brain. If she had it her way, she would simply never leave her bedroom again.

"The horses...," she thought, knowing they needed to be fed.

After watching Liam drive away, she had beelined for the house, taking the back way in so she could avoid the stares of her friends and every person Cathy knew in Florida. Locking herself in her room, Emma had heard Cathy come in an hour later, but she had gone directly downstairs. It made her physically nauseous to know what she had done to her on such an important day.

How could she have been so selfish?

Last night had been nothing short of mortifying in every way.

Emma wondered if Michael had been injured when he hit that fence. If it was hard enough to crack the wood, it had to have hurt.

Emma rolled over to look at her phone. The only message she had was from Mandy, who had said something about how she would get through this. Emma half smiled at her friend's thoughtful gesture. After processing what had happened last night, she had called her best friend and told her every detail. Mandy may be hundreds or thousands of miles away at any given time, (depending on where she was traveling for work that week), but she still remained the kind of friend she could call up when things hit the fan. Every time they spoke on the phone, no matter how long it had been since the last call, it was as if no time had passed at all.

Talking to Mandy had helped, but nothing was going to take away from the fact that today was going to be rough, to say the least. Emma may have been able to run away from her problems last night, but today she was going to have to face them head on whether she liked it or not.

Groaning, she slid off the bed and pulled on a pair of shorts and a tank top. Emma looked at herself in the mirror, cringing at her puffy, still red eyes no thanks to the crying and the little sleep she'd gotten. Pulling her hair into a ponytail, she headed towards her bedroom door, hesitating before she opened it.

Emma padded quietly down the hall, relieved to see Cathy was not yet awake. She knew she would have to face her soon, but first thing this morning wouldn't have been ideal.

The horses nickered as she slid the barn door open, the only ones on this farm oblivious to last night's drama. Michael was either not up yet or was elsewhere on the farm, and she was glad she could at least feed the horses while processing her thoughts. Before heading to the feed room, she walked over to Valentine's stall and leaned her forehead against her mare's. Valentine blew out soft, slow breaths, calming her soul in a way nothing else in the world could. She breathed in and out slowly with her eyes closed, sucking in the familiar sounds and smells of the horses. Giving her mare a quick pat, she headed to the feed room.

"Hey, Em," Michael's voice said softly, making her jump. Between the sound of horses eager to get their breakfast and the loud sound of grain hitting the buckets, Emma didn't hear Michael creak down the flight of stairs next to the barn like she usually did.

Emma turned around, scanning his remorseful expression.

"Are you ok?" she asked, her voice barely above a whisper.

"A little bruised, but I'm alright," Michael said, half shrugging. "Are you?" he added.

"I don't...I don't know," she stammered, carrying the first stack of buckets towards the horses' stalls, dumping them into the feed bins. Michael grabbed the other stack she had already prepared, feeding the horses on the opposite side. They didn't speak again until the horses were all munching quietly on their grain.

Emma opened the hay room door, putting a bale of hay in her wheelbarrow as she headed down the aisle to throw them each some flakes. She wanted to know what happened after she left the party, but in a way, she also didn't want to know.

"Ignorance is bliss," she thought.

"What happened with Liam, before he left, I mean," Michael asked tentatively. Emma supposed he had a right to know what went down on her end; after all, he did get tossed into a wooden fence for it.

She paused after throwing a flake of hay to the next horse, turning to face him. "I'm so sorry Michael. I couldn't take it anymore. I had to tell him," she replied, shooting him an apologetic look before continuing down the aisle, throwing hay into the last few stalls.

"Don't be. I deserved it. I messed up and my actions had consequences." Michael's eyes shifted down to the floor. Emma felt torn now, between Michael's guilt and Liam's heartbreak over what Michael did. It had been a moment of weakness, an impulsion, and she knew he felt bad. But seeing the look on Michael's face now, she didn't quite know to what extent.

"Did Liam forgive you? I mean...are you guys ok?" Michael asked, his eyes meeting hers again.

"I don't think so. He said he wanted to take a break," Emma said, turning to put the wheelbarrow away.

"What does that mean?" Michael replied.

"Your guess is as good as mine," she said, shaking her head.

That was the million dollar question.

Now, Emma's curiosity outweighed wanting to stay ignorant about what happened after she and Liam left a crowd of people gawking after them.

"What happened after we left the party?" she asked, turning back around.

"Well, it was awkward, to say the least. Sam helped me up, and then up the stairs to my apartment so I could ice down where I landed. Before we went upstairs, everyone started murmuring about what they thought happened, and Cathy...well she just looked mortified."

Emma's heart sank at the thought.

"Before I made it to the stairs, she seemed to snap out of it though, and asked the DJ to turn the music up, I'm guessing, because a much louder upbeat song came on a couple seconds later. When I was about to head into my apartment, I glanced down and everyone seemed to be going back to normal from what I could tell," he added, seeing the bleak look on Emma's face.

"I don't even know what to say to her," Emma said, still processing that information. It hadn't crossed her mind until now, but when Cathy learned the truth, would she fire Michael? It made her sick to think about her actions causing pain for so many people.

Michael gave her a sympathetic look, clearly unsure of what to say. What could he say anyway?

After that, Emma continued on with her morning chores and Sam arrived shortly after her conversation with Michael had ended. He greeted them both but seemed to walk on eggshells for most of the morning. Emma couldn't blame him; he probably didn't know how to react after everything that went down.

She tried her best to act casual, like nothing happened, for his sake. The last thing she wanted was their brand-new employee to feel uncomfortable in his new work environment.

"What a disaster," she thought periodically as the morning drug on. Normally, Emma would go back to the house to make and

eat her own breakfast after the horses had theirs. Today, she would much rather starve then have to look Cathy in the eye after what she did.

Eventually, Emma knew she would have to go back in the house and face her. But for now, she was happy living off the bag of chips she had stolen from Michael's apartment. He had offered her more, but it felt wrong somehow given the situation at hand.

The time had come. She literally could not avoid going home any longer. Emma was dizzy with hunger, and she had completed her work and then some for the day.

When Emma finally went back to the house for the night, she sighed with relief when she saw Cathy's car wasn't parked outside. A note was left on the kitchen counter in her handwriting, though.

Emma,

Went to dinner with a friend. See you later this evening.

– Cathy

The relief she felt was quickly replaced with the anxiety that at some random point in the evening, Cathy would be walking through the front door forcing Emma to talk to her about what happened. Could she simply go to bed early and pretend she was tired?

That seemed like the ideal option, but it would only cause the anxious feeling in her gut to build the more time drug on.

It was time to be a big girl and face the consequences of her own actions.

Emma sat on the couch after pouring an exceptionally tall glass of wine and flipped through channels mindlessly. Nothing on TV seemed to interest her; at least nothing that would keep her attention away from her thoughts. By the time she heard the front doorknob turn, she had run through a hundred possible ways the conversation with Cathy could go.

At this point, Emma just wanted to rip off the band-aid and see if anyone was fired or if Cathy was going to hate her forever.

"Hi Cathy," Emma said weakly as she stood up to greet her.

Cathy smiled at her, but the typical warmth in her eyes wasn't there.

"How much does she know?" Emma thought, feeling a wave of nausea hit her stomach again.

"Can we walk?" Emma added, as Cathy set down her purse.

"Of course, dear," Cathy said, but her voice didn't ring with its typical enthusiasm. Cathy walked across the room and took a seat on the chair that sat across from the couch. Emma sat back down; standing didn't seem appropriate for a conversation like this.

Before Emma could say anything, Cathy spoke again.

"Emma, what happened last night?"

"Did Liam really not tell her by now?" she thought.

Somehow that made this conversation worse. Why had he not called his aunt and explained what happened? Was he that angry and upset? Could she blame him?

"Cathy, I want to tell you how sorry I am your party was ruined. The way it all happened...well, it shouldn't have happened that way," Emma said.

Cathy's confused gaze bore into her. Cathy still didn't understand why Liam reacted the way he did, and there was no way to dance around the facts any longer.

"A few months ago, Michael kissed me. It was, well, brief and it meant nothing. He just had too much to drink and it just...happened," Emma stammered, biting her lip a moment to control her emotions before she proceeded.

"I should have told Liam right away, but I didn't. Nothing has happened between Michael and I since. We are just friends, and I didn't want to hurt Liam, but I just could not take lying to him a second longer...," Emma's voice broke as her emotions overtook her.

Cathy suddenly stood up and walked across the living room, taking a seat next to Emma.

"My dear, a kiss never means nothing," Cathy said softly, sighing and placing one hand on her shoulder.

Emma wasn't sure what to say to that. It had meant nothing though, hadn't it? At least, that's what Michael had said and what she had been letting herself believe.

"I care about Liam, I do. And I don't want anything to come between you and I, Cathy, or my job at this farm...I...," Emma's voice broke again, and sobs rattled her body now. The emotions she had been bottling up the last twenty-four hours were finally coming to the surface. The exposed truth was overwhelming her. Emma still feared for her and Michael's jobs now that Cathy knew everything.

Cathy looked at her sympathetically. What was Cathy going to say?

"Emma, I was twenty-something once too, you know. Relationships at that age, well, they are hard. You're in the middle of so much change and learning to be an adult in the real world for the first time. I would be naïve to think that you and Liam won't go through rough patches or even not end up together in the end. While nothing would make me happier to see my nephew end up with a young woman like you, I also want *you* to be happy. If that's with Liam or Michael or someone else, I hope you understand that I have come to care for you as a daughter regardless. I meant what I said when I asked you to run this farm, and if you and Liam are no longer together, well, that changes nothing about our business relationship or how I feel about you," Cathy said.

Emma looked up, suddenly feeling a little less panicked than she had thirty seconds ago.

"And Michael?" Emma croaked, still partially fearing for his job too.

"Michael is an excellent employee. While I wish what happened last night hadn't happened, I am certainly not letting a good employee go based on this one personal incident. Even if it did involve my nephew," Cathy replied.

It felt like a ten-ton weight had been lifted off her chest. No one was fired, and Cathy didn't seem to completely hate her either.

Although, she knew it may never be quite the same between her and Cathy if she and Liam didn't make it through this break.

So really, that only left one problem: where exactly did she stand with Liam? And what was it she wanted? The kiss with Michael had only been one problem of two; they still lived over three hours apart and had busy careers that put an incredible strain on their relationship.

Cathy stood back up, interrupting her churning mind. She walked over to the fridge, pulling out a fresh bottle of wine and grabbed a glass from the wine rack. Bringing both the bottle and her glass back to the living room, Cathy poured the wine into Emma's empty glass from earlier and her new one and set the bottle on the coffee table.

"It's safe to say we could both use a little wine tonight," Cathy said, offering Emma a smile and the glass that was filled quite a bit more than a traditional restaurant pour.

Emma smiled back, wiping the last of her tears from her puffy eyes. Picking the remote back up from where it lay on the couch's arm rest, she turned it to the movie channel.

In no time, the two were laughing along with an old chick flick, and for a moment, Emma let herself pretend the last twenty-four hours hadn't happened at all.

Chapter Eleven

Valentine jigged in place and Emma circled in front of the start box for the third time. They were next to go on the cross country course, and her mare had made it clear she was tired of waiting.

"Easy," Emma murmured to the mare, running her fingers up her neck softly as she spoke. Valentine had learned all too quickly what the start box meant, and she didn't like being told to wait her turn.

"Ten seconds," the volunteer told her, smiling sympathetically at Emma as she walked her horse in yet another circle to keep her from charging through the start box prematurely.

"Three...two...one...have a great ride!"

Emma didn't need to ask, as usual, and her mare broke into an open canter the moment she let the reins slide ever so slightly through her hands.

"Thank you!" Emma called over her shoulder as they galloped out into the open field towards the rolltop in front of them. Her horse took a long spot, eagerly launching over the jump with a little more room to spare than she needed. Emma had been worried about moving up Val to novice level since she felt they had just finally got a handle on dressage at the beginner novice level. But the way her mare charged down those smaller fences, she figured a little extra height might actually help her horse back off a bit and make her pay attention to her a little more.

So far, that theory was already out the window. Three cross country fences in, and the mare was making it clear she had zero fear, despite the increase in jump height.

"All gas and no brake today," Emma murmured under her breath as they took the next fence on course out of stride, perhaps still taking a little bit of a long spot despite her efforts to try and come into a deeper distance.

Emma had to admit, her horse had done better in dressage after moving up a level than she'd anticipated. Although, she still expected to see the word "tense" written in several boxes on their score card. At least she was trying, (and no longer jumping out of the dressage ring), which is all Emma could really ask of her.

It had been one week since the night of the grand opening party that threw life as she knew it out of whack. Mainly, she was just glad that there didn't seem to be any awkwardness between her and Cathy, or Cathy and Michael for that matter.

Flying across the cross country course, she enjoyed the feeling of the rest of the world simply vanishing when she was out here. It was just her and Valentine, and nothing else mattered.

Including the fact that Liam hadn't called her once since the night of the grand opening party. Emma understood, of course. It had only been a week, and he needed time to process. Still, this weird relationship limbo left a sick feeling in her stomach every time she thought about it. Which until today, was far too often.

Valentine dropped into the water without hesitation; a first for her. Her horse had slowly been getting less intimidated by water she couldn't see the bottom of. Today, however, Emma felt a confidence in her mare that had come with the endless practice sessions at home and mileage at other shows.

Emma had briefly considered not competing this weekend, fearing her head wouldn't be in the right place. But after her talk with Cathy, she decided to dive headlong into her work at the farm and preparing her horse for this eventing trial instead. Clearly, her ultra-focus this week had paid off.

As they crossed the finish flags, Emma beamed down at her horse; they had pulled off a double clear round.

Michael stood at the edge of the field, and Emma could see him cheering for them as she pulled her horse up to a walk.

"Looks like you guys had fun," Michael said, patting Valentine, whose nostrils flared. Still, Val kept trying to break into a trot in spite of Emma's almost constant reminder to keep walking.

Emma laughed at the mare, who despite her heavy breaths and coat covered in sweat, acted like she hadn't just galloped around an entire cross country course.

"Aren't you tired, lady?" Emma asked, shaking her head as she asked Valentine to walk once again. Catching a strange look on Michael's face, she held his gaze, titling her head.

"What?" she asked, curious what secret he was keeping behind those green eyes. Emma knew him well enough to know when he was hiding something.

"Well...she made me promise not to tell you," Michael stammered, looking away from her.

"She? Who made you promise?" Emma pressed, even more curious now.

"Mandy...she stopped by the farm this morning. She was planning to surprise you, but we were already at the horse show. Anyway, Sam told her where you would be and...," Michael began.

"Mandy is *here*?!" Emma replied, cutting him off mid-sentence, her jaw dropping a little.

Mandy? How long had it been since she had seen her best friend from back home in person? Since the day they packed up their apartment and Emma drove to Florida? How had so much time passed? So much had changed since she last saw her friend. Sure, they still talked on the phone fairly frequently, but talking and seeing her one another in person were two very different things.

Emma recalled Mandy saying she had some vacation time built up as she hadn't taken a real vacation since she started this job. Still, Emma hadn't expected her to drop everything and come visit. Not that she was complaining; a visit from her best friend was exactly what she needed in her life right now. Really, the timing couldn't be more perfect.

"Where is she?" Emma asked, eager to reunite with her friend.

"Back at the show stables. Apparently, she did some asking around at the show office and they pointed her in the right direction. Mandy saw me at our stalls and asked about you right after you left for cross country warm-up. I told her who I was and then I almost didn't make it over here to watch your round because she had a lot of questions," Michael said, chuckling a little.

Emma laughed; that didn't surprise her one bit. Mandy knew far too much about Michael but had never met him in person. Poor Michael!

"I'm going to walk Val out and head that way. See you back at the stalls." Emma replied.

"See you!" Michael said as she walked off.

"Mandy," Emma thought again, still a little bit in disbelief she was about to see her best friend for the first time in almost a year.

Emma took the long loop around the field that led to the barns so her horse would be cooled down by the time she reached them. Emma squinted her eyes against the sun trying to make out the figure sitting on a tack box where her stalls were located.

Before Emma was all the way down the aisle, Mandy spotted her and Valentine, and jogged over to them as she called out her name. Seeing Mandy, it was as if they hadn't spent a minute apart.

"Mandy!" Emma exclaimed, sliding off Valentine's side as they all but collided into a hug. "I can't believe you're here!"

"Well, I had some vacation time to burn and it seemed like you needed a friend right now," Mandy said, hugging her again.

"*I really did though,*" Emma thought.

"Are you done for the day?" Mandy asked, patting Valentine on the neck. Valentine lipped at Mandy's pockets, hoping she was hiding treats for her in there. Mandy smiled, showing the mare her empty shorts pockets. Valentine sniffed them once more to be safe, turning her attention elsewhere when she realized Mandy had no horse cookies for her.

"I have my show jumping round in a couple hours, but then I'm done for the day!" Emma replied.

"Good, that means we have time to catch up," Mandy said, following Emma as she led her horse back to the barns.

After Valentine was hosed off and put away, Emma and Mandy sat side by side on her tack box, catching up on what was going on in Mandy's world. It was a nice change of pace from talking about her own issues.

Too soon, it was time for Emma to tack her horse back up and get ready for their stadium jumping round. They were sitting in sixth place right now, and a good stadium round could really launch her into a higher placing.

After a quick warm-up, Emma stood near the entry gate waiting for her turn. Michael hung his arms over the fence surrounding the ring and Mandy had her back leaning against it, talking his ear off again.

Emma smirked; it was funny seeing two people from two very different parts of her life getting to know each other. Well, mostly Mandy getting to know Michael. Poor Michael hardly had time to say anything except the answers to the many questions he was being drilled with.

"You ready?" The lady at the gate asked as she was swinging it open, letting out the person who had just been on course.

"Yes, thank you!"

Emma walked Valentine into the empty ring. It was starting to get dark now, and the flood lights had kicked on a couple riders ago. There was something about competing at dusk when they turned the lights on that made her feel like a professional rider. Probably because most of the big shows were held at night, under the lights.

The buzzer sounded, queuing her horse to canter before she had a chance to. Emma circled, getting the mare to focus and relax the best she could before pointing her at the first fence.

To Emma, nothing in this world compared to being on course with this mare. Whether it be show jumping or cross country, Valentine's love of jumping was contagious. It drowned out everything else.

In her hyper focus on horse show prep and work this week, Emma felt like they had really prepared themselves for this moment. Valentine's ears flicked forward and back as she focused on the jump and Emma's voice simultaneously. They sailed over the first jump with enthusiasm, and Valentine landed and waited for Emma to tell her which direction she would be turning, like they had practiced at home. It was much improved from the way she used to land and bolt.

"One...two...three...four...," Emma said, counting aloud as they cantered down the outside line. She turned her head, feeling Valentine shift under her as she anticipated a sharp rollback turn. The practice they had been putting in lately was paying off already.

"Three...two...one...," Emma thought, counting down the strides to the very large and impressive oxer ahead of them.

"Last fence...don't stop riding!" she thought, trying to keep her head in the game.

Valentine seemed to sense the end of the course was near, and it never helped when a last fence was in the direct path of the out gate. She felt her horse's muscles bunch beneath her as she started to leave the ground a stride early. There was nothing Emma could do now but get out of her mare's way and hope for the best.

Valentine tucked her legs underneath her neatly; she hated taking down rails and seemed to revel in her own power as she cleared the fence with room to spare despite the long spot. This horse knew she had two jobs on course; go fast and keep the rails up.

Emma beamed as all four of her horse's hooves hit the ground; had they really just pulled off another clean round today? That was surely going to put them close to the top of the leaderboard. Michael and Mandy were clapping and cheering from the sidelines as she exited the show ring.

For the first time all week, the drama of last week's party and her failing relationship with Liam were far from her mind.

But that's the thing about horsewomen, isn't it? You just can't keep them beat down for long.

"So, the TSA guy asks me, what's in this bag? Rocks? I was like well, actually yes, they are beach rocks for my mom's beach themed bathroom!" Mandy said, taking another sip of her wine and laughing.

Emma laughed too at the best story Mandy had told all night about her traveling job. It had been far too long since the two of them sat on a front porch with a glass of wine laughing like this.

What a day it had been; between a successful day placing second in their division at the eventing trial and Mandy's surprise visit, it just didn't get any better than this.

Mandy pulled the bottle of wine from the portable wine cooler it was in and topped off both of their glasses.

"I've missed you, my friend," Mandy said, clinking her glass against Emma's.

"I've missed you too," Emma replied.

They both looked out across the rolling hills and the sun setting behind them, enjoying the cool, late evening sky.

"So, Michael is nice," Mandy said, shooting her friend a mischievous look.

"Yes, he's a great friend," Emma said, taking another sip of her wine as she prepared herself for what she knew would only be the first of many Michael versus Liam questions.

"A friend, huh? Is that why he kissed you?" Mandy asked in a sarcastic tone.

"I mean, he said it was a mistake...," Emma began, but Mandy was already turning around in her chair ready to drill her with more questions.

"Yeah sure, but that's because he felt bad about the timing of the kiss, but I saw the way he looks at you, Emma," Mandy said, cutting her off.

"And how exactly do you think he is looking at me?" Emma asked, shooting Mandy a look that said she didn't buy it.

"Like he wants to kiss you again," Mandy replied, scooting closer and giving Emma a smirk and wink.

Well, Emma had suspected all along that Michael had feelings for her, hadn't she? This shouldn't exactly be breaking news. Still, Emma remembered the picture of Jane on his nightstand and her suspicions he wasn't ready to move on from that.

Emma replied by spilling the story of how she had stumbled upon his late fiancé's photo in his apartment. Mandy paused, processing the information Emma had shared.

"I mean, maybe he just wants her memory to live on, you know? And not feel like he's forgetting her by hiding her picture? Anyway, none of that matters unless you know how you feel about him. I know you're technically on a break with Liam, but at some point, you're going to have to figure out what *you* want. Are you going to do your best to get Liam back and make it work long distance, really committing to that? Or are you going to explore your feelings for Michael and officially end things with Liam? *If* you have feelings for Michael that is," Mandy said.

Emma had never really let herself explore feelings with Michael as an option. When she had started at Twin Oaks, she was focused on her internship, and dating her co-worker was not an option. Then, she ran into Liam, started dating, and was committed to him.

But now, with things up in the air with Liam and Mandy asking her questions she couldn't avoid...what was it she actually wanted?

"Honestly Mandy...I don't even know," Emma said, meeting her friend's gaze, a puzzled expression crossing her face.

Yes, there was certainly a lot to consider now that things had changed.

—ele—

Emma turned off the TV; she couldn't take hearing the words "possibility of a tornado" or "severe storm warning" one more time.

Instead, she wanted to see what else she could do to help Michael and Sam prepare the house and the barn for what was coming. And from what the Ocala weather channel folks had to say, it wasn't good.

This was the first time Emma had experienced any kind of severe weather since this farm had become her responsibility, and with Cathy back in Wellington, the horses' safety fell entirely on her. And that was a responsibility she took seriously.

Mandy could be heard on a business call, despite being on vacation, in the spare bedroom. Emma wasn't surprised about it – Mandy lived for her job.

Emma strode across the grass blowing softly in the wind. The breeze was a little stronger today than normal and the skies were partly cloudy, but nothing about today's weather gave away the storm brewing somewhere in the distance.

Emma could hear the sound of a power screwdriver turning over against metal as she entered the barn. Michael paused, wiping sweat from his brow, then gave it a few more turns before he seemed satisfied with it and moved onto the next one.

"Making sure no horse stall latches are loose this time?" Emma teased, recalling that fateful night that Jimmie John has escaped due to a faulty latch.

"You know it! As much fun as it was chasing down a horse in the pouring rain, I'd prefer not to do it again," Michael said, sarcasm in his voice. Clearly, he had the same thought she did.

"Anything else I can do to help?" Emma asked.

"We got most of it at this point. Sam is checking fence boards to make sure nothing is loose that could be pulled off by the wind, so really all that's left is securing the jumps in the arena," he replied.

"Let's do it!" Emma replied, heading to the arena.

Michael and Emma began taking jump standards and laying them on the ground so the wind wouldn't knock them down and break them. Emma looked over at Michael as he stacked some of the lighter standards together. But this time, unlike in the past, she let herself *really look* at him.

Not that she hadn't noticed that he was attractive before. Of course she had. But Emma wasn't that kind of girl, and with the barriers of being strictly co-workers, and then being with Liam, she had never really let her mind go there. But now, with Mandy's words asking her what she wanted bouncing around her thoughts, she did.

Michael *was* incredibly attractive to her. She recalled the first day she met him, thinking that he was very much her type. Not only that, but he was also her best friend now, and you know what they say about familiarity being attractive. Still, was she ready to throw away everything with Liam for a what if? Liam who loved her and who would still be with her today if he hadn't found out about the kiss?

Emma signed audibly. Maybe she needed more time to see where she even stood with Liam. He had finally sent her a message asking her how she was, and she had responded with news of Mandy's arrival and the placing at the horse show in which he had sent a congratulations back. But other than that very short conversation, they hadn't really talked. As each day passed, Emma wondered more and more about where they stood.

By the time they were done securing the jumps, the heat and humidity had taken their toll. She swore she could feel the moisture in the air getting thicker as each minute passed: a telltale sign the storm was in fact coming. Emma told Michael to have Sam finish up anything necessary for storm prep and to head home. She wanted to be sure he had ample time to get home safely and prepare his own home for what was coming.

Michael helped Emma feed, tossing a few extra flakes of hay so the horses would be distracted, and double check everything one last time.

"Well, I guess that's all we can do," Emma said.

"Don't worry, I'll be right above the barn if anything goes sideways," Michael said, catching Emma's worried look as her eyes passed over the horses munching contently on their grain.

"If it gets bad out here, come to the house and camp out in the basement," Emma said, giving him a worried look.

"I will. Don't worry too much though. They always hype up summer storms like this. They typically come and go quickly," Michael added.

"I'll try," Emma said, only half convinced after watching far too much of the weather channel on her lunch break.

"See you in the morning," Michael said.

"Goodnight," Emma said, closing the barn doors as she headed back to the house.

Glancing at the sky one more time, she saw the clouds had become significantly darker in just the last hour alone. A gust of wind blew through her hair, sweeping it across her face.

Emma tried to remind herself this wasn't the first storm these horses had encountered, and she was probably being overly worried because of her new responsibilities as barn manager.

She could only hope that Michael was right.

Emma didn't mean to fall asleep on the couch.

In fact, she had every intention of staying up so she could keep a close eye on the weather. The last thing she wanted was the rude awakening she was getting right now; the sound of sirens in the distance and the wind whipping tree branches against the side of her house.

Her eyes flew open, locking in on the TV that was still on. The weatherman was mid-sentence, talking about high winds and the tornado watch that had just turned into a warning.

The door to the spare room Mandy was staying in creaked open and Emma heard her padding down the hallway behind her.

"Are those sirens?" Mandy asked groggily.

"Yeah, they woke me up too," Emma said, sitting up and stretching. Mandy plopped onto the couch next to Emma, laying her head against the pillow on her right.

"Is it bad enough we need to go to the basement, or can we go back to bed?" Mandy asked, still sounding half asleep.

"I'm not sure…," Emma began before she was interrupted by her phone ringing on the coffee table in front of them.

"Michael? That can't be good," she thought, picking up the phone.

"Emma? I think we have a problem. It's Manny; he's freaking out and I can't get him to calm down. He was pretty restless before, but once the sirens started going off, he just lost it," Michael said, worry leaking into his tone.

Emma was already standing straight up, fully awake now.

"I'll be right there," Emma replied, hanging up the phone.

"You aren't going out there are you?! Em, they just said there's a funnel cloud ten miles from here. We really should get to the basement," Mandy said, throwing her friend a worried look. But Emma was already pulling on her rubber boots by the front door.

"I can't leave Manny in this state. He needs my help, or he could really hurt himself. I'll be back as soon as I can and will bring Michael with me. Keep an eye on the news for me, ok?" Emma replied, one hand already on the doorknob.

"Ok…just be careful," Mandy said, her eyebrows raised with concern.

"I will," Emma said, opening the door and closing it quickly behind her.

Two steps away from the door and a strong gust of wind came from her left, threatening to knock her off balance. Her long hair flew in front of her eyes blinding her momentarily until she pulled it away, only to have it whipped back against her cheek again moments later.

Wishing she had taken the time to grab a hair tie, Emma pushed on, half blind, as she made her way across the familiar ground. Luckily, she could walk from the house to the barn all but blindfolded.

While it was only spitting rain right now, the wind blasted the large rain drops into her, stinging any exposed skin as she continued on.

Squinting against the wind, rain, and her own hair still whipping into her, she tried opening the barn door as quietly as possible so she wouldn't spook poor Manny any more than he already was. Emma slid through the crack in the door that was just big enough for her to get through and quickly shut the door behind her.

Manny's eyes were wide with the whites of his eyes visible as he stared at Emma and the partially opened barn door that allowed him to catch a glimpse of the storm outside. Manny panic snorted, his nostril flaring widely, and he circled his stall several times. He almost appeared to be a different color because he was so drenched in sweat.

The other horses looked alarmed and wide-eyed too, mostly staring at the panicked Manny, but were otherwise ok.

Emma and Michael exchanged a concerned look. She gave Valentine a quick pet as she headed to Manny's stall, although her mare seemed fairly unfazed by the creaking barn around her.

"Easy, Manny, it's ok buddy," Emma murmured to the gelding, who had his eyes locked on her, trembling when he stood still. Dialing the number on his stall card, Emma tried calling his owner.

"Shoot!" she said, trying again since she hadn't answered. After one text message and another call, Emma put her phone in her pocket. It looked like she was going to be on her own as far as making a decision to help this poor, terrified older horse.

"Poor guy seems to have some pretty bad storm anxiety, huh?" Michael said, looking at the gelding who was circling in his stall again.

"I hate giving horses medication without owner approval, especially since Manny is so new to us," Emma said, shaking her head as she headed toward the feed room. Pulling a bag of calming herbs that she liked using on her mare before competitions, she mixed the maximum dose in with a handful of grain and headed back to Manny's stall. Thunder cracked in the distance, causing Manny to spook again and fly backwards, bumping into the back of his stall, scaring himself once more.

"Come on Manny, it's ok," Emma said shaking the grain bucket in front of him now. Manny reached out and sniffed the grain, pulling his nose away quickly and circling his stall. Emma dumped the grain into his feed bin, hoping he would eat it there. He quickly sniffed it and turned his nose away, ears pricked in the distance of the thunder, trembling again.

Emma sighed loudly, slumping against the side of the barn wall. Michael walked over to where she was, leaning against the same wall and rested a hand on her shoulder.

"What else can we do for him?" Michael asked quietly.

"I think he needs a sedative. I just wish I could get ahold of his owner to get it approved first. An herbal supplement isn't a huge deal, but a sedative is a different story. His owner mentioned in his notes when Manny arrived that he sometimes gets a little storm anxiety, but I think a storm this bad just has him worked up more than normal," Emma said as she shook her head, watching the horse trembling in the corner again. The storm was going to be getting worse before it got better, and it made Emma sick to think about leaving him in this condition when they would finally have to head to the basement.

Standing up, she headed back to the medicine cabinet in the feed room and pulled a bottle of sedative and a fresh syringe off the shelf. Emma knew at some point in her position as a barn manager she would have to make some executive decisions regarding a horse's care, especially when an owner couldn't be reached. She just didn't expect to have to make one quite so soon.

Between classes at college and working for Maggie and Twin Oaks, Emma had dosed plenty of horses with this particular sedative. Still, it made her uneasy doing it without owner consent. But at this point, it didn't seem like she had another option.

"Michael, can you put his halter on for me and see if you can get him to stand as still as possible?"

Michael nodded, doing his best to slide the halter over the gelding's head as gingerly as possible. Manny, the old gentleman he was, let Michael halter him but danced around on the end of the lead rope a little after that. Emma flicked the syringe with her other hand, clearing it of air bubbles as she prepped the injection.

"Ok bud, just stand still for me for two seconds, all right? This is going to make you feel a lot better," Emma cooed to him, walking over to his head and neck slowly. Emma ran her hand across his sweat-drenched coat several times, until his skin didn't flinch under her touch. Finding the best spot within the triangular area on his neck where she had been taught to do intramuscular injections, she quickly plunged the needle in. Swiftly plunging the liquid into his neck, she capped the needle and put her hand on the area she injected.

"That's a good boy, Manny, you're so brave," she murmured soothingly. Truth be told he was so distracted by the storm raging outside he hardly noticed the injection at all.

"Ok, you can take his halter off. Thanks," Emma told Michael in a hushed tone. He quickly slid the halter off, and they stepped out of the stall. Emma walked back over to the other side of the barn aisle and slid down the stall, sitting cross-legged on the ground in front of Valentine's stall where she had a direct view of Manny. Michael walked over and sat next to her a few feet away. The barn around them creaked and groaned as the wind swirled around outside. The rain on the tin roof above them sounded louder now.

"The storm must be moving closer," she thought.

"How long will it take for the sedative to kick in?" Michael asked, watching Manny snort and tremble still.

"Usually between fifteen and thirty minutes. Hopefully sooner than later for poor Manny's sake," Emma replied.

Pulling her phone out of her pocket, Emma glanced at the message on the screen.

"Em, you guys should get back here; the storm is getting worse," Mandy's text message read.

"Mandy?" Michael asked, seeing the look on Emma's face as she read the message.

"Yeah, she's worried about us. I'm not leaving Manny until the sedative kicks in though. I have to know he isn't going to injure himself before it does since the storm is only getting worse. If you want to head to the house now you can though," Emma replied.

"No way. I'm staying here with you," he said, his eyes meeting hers as he held her gaze. Michael cared for her; that much was crystal clear in those intense green eyes. Emma felt a small flutter in her stomach as she continued to stare back at him.

"Have you been doing ok? After, well, everything with Liam?" Michael added.

"Better than I was at first. Mostly now I just hate this feeling of being in relationship limbo and not knowing where we stand. We've hardly spoken since that night at the party, and I just feel like I want to either work things out or move on," Emma replied, still holding Michael's gaze.

Michael tilted his head slightly, scanning her expression. What was he thinking?

"Do you want to get back together with Liam?" Michael asked.

Ah there it was, the million dollar question. The one she been pondering since she and Liam took this break in the first place. As each day passed though, and the heartbreak of separating was less intense than the last, it replaced the heart-wrenching feeling with clarity. The clarity that she had been struggling with the long distance between them for a while now and the fact that they simply lived separate lives. Still, Emma felt somehow tied to Liam and felt a pang of guilt for wanting to give up on everything they did have once. She still cared about him too; she was still attracted to him, and she missed him sometimes. But was that enough for her to wait around for Liam or keep going the way they had before?

"I'm not sure," she replied. "Honestly, I was struggling with how little we saw of each other because of our busy lives and the long distance before the break," Emma admitted.

"I could tell it was taking its toll on you," Michael said, a look of sympathy on his face. Had she really been that obvious about her feelings? Or was it Michael simply knew her that well? Maybe a little of both.

"It was rough being so far away and trying to maintain a relationship sometimes," she replied.

Michael's eyes flitted away momentarily as he placed his hand on top of hers, meeting her gaze again when they touched.

"I hope you know I'm always here for you if you need me," he said softly, his eyes still locked into hers.

"I know, and thank you," Emma said, her voice barely above a whisper. She wondered if he heard her above the sounds of the storm outside and the creaking barn.

Michael's body leaned in slowly, so slowly she didn't even know he was getting closer at first. His hand ran up her arm and gently rested on the side of her cheek. He was still looking into her eyes, his own conveying an unspoken message.

It was then that Emma finally knew without a shadow of a doubt: Michael had feelings for her.

The loud sound of a horse's body thudding against the ground caught her attention, and she turned her head. Michael's hand pulled back and he turned around toward the sound as well.

Manny was laying on the ground, his legs curled up under him like a cat, his lower lip hanging lazily. His eyes were blinking, closing for half a second as he fought sleep. Emma smiled at the now relaxed horse.

"I think the sedative kicked in," she said at a whisper still.

"We should probably head to the house then," Michael replied, listening to the intensity of the storm outside.

"Let's go," she said in a hushed tone.

They shut off the barn lights and slid the barn door open, exposing the ominous looking night sky. Emma shut and latched the barn door quickly so she wouldn't spook the horses unnecessarily. For a moment, Michael and Emma stood under the overhang that was sheltering them from the rain, preparing themselves to run through the raging storm only inches away.

Michael looked over at Emma and held out his hand, offering her to take it.

"Ready?" he asked, looking over at her.

Emma hesitated a half second and then placed her hand in his.

"Ready," she stated, looking at him and then back out in front of them.

They ran headlong into the wind and rain, which was much more intense than it had been when she first came out to the barn. Emma was forced to shut her eyes and run blind for a moment as the rain pelted into her face, thankful she had grabbed Michael's hand. Wind whipped past her ears making a howling sound as they ran on.

By the time they reached the covered front porch they were both soaked to the bone. Emma's hair hung in wet, matted clumps against her neck. Michael took his baseball hat off briefly, shaking it off and exposing his soaking wet hair too before putting it back on his head.

He turned to face Emma, looking at her soaking wet frame and began laughing his typical deep laugh. Emma laughed too seeing what he saw; they looked a little like wet cats.

She realized in that moment that they were still holding hands. Her eyes flitted to her hand in his and he released it reflexively.

"Sorry," he said, his expression reflecting his feelings and perhaps a little hurt that maybe Emma had implied she was uncomfortable still holding his hand.

Emma's mind stopped processing logic as she continued to stare at him. For once she wasn't overthinking. She wasn't weighing the pros and cons of chasing down her failed relationship with Liam. She wasn't thinking about the drama their previous kiss had caused them a week ago or the months of strain it put on their friendship prior to that.

The only thing she was thinking about was how much she cared about Michael. How she had felt a sense of safety and trust since the first storm that brought them together so many months ago. How he had put his own life at risk to protect her more than once. How he was not only her best friend but someone she had realized some time ago that she wanted to be permanently part of her life no matter what changed. And now, how much she was attracted to him in a way she had never let herself consider.

Yes, logic had taken a backseat to the emotions welling up inside her. Perhaps it was the sleep deprivation and pouring rain next to them that had something to do with it, but either way, she saw Michael through new eyes tonight.

Emma took one step towards Michael, closing the gap between them. Her eyes locked onto his, only inches from his face now. Michael's eyes widened slightly in surprise, and she read a little confusion in his expression. Could she blame him? She had never crossed a line like this before.

Her mind buzzed. But the voice in the back of her head that normally told her all the reasons that what she was about to do was a bad idea was silent. Emma slowly reached her hand up toward Michael's flushed cheek, gently making contact with his still damp skin. She slowly leaned in closer, and Michael responded by doing the same.

Their lips touched and unlike the last time, they lingered there. His arm wrapped around the hollow of her waist as he pulled her in closer and they stood there, closer than they had ever been, kissing as the rain pounded around them inches away. A gust of wind tore through a nearby tree, causing the leaves to rattle against each other loudly.

Emma gently pulled away after a few moments, locking eyes with Michael one more time. She smiled warmly at him, taking a step back.

"We better head inside," Emma said, shooting a glance at the storm still worsening by the minute.

"We probably should," Michael said, although his hand was still wrapped around her waist, and he made no movement toward the front door.

A crack of loud thunder made them both jump, signaling them to turn simultaneously toward the house. They stepped through the front door still dripping wet, and Mandy turned around in surprise from where she was still sitting on the couch.

"Finally! I thought you guys got blown away," Mandy teased, standing up and looking them both up and down. She disappeared down the hallway and returned with a couple towels, tossing them at Emma and Michael.

"Ok, now that I know you're alive, I'm going downstairs to the basement," Mandy said sarcastically, winking at Emma.

"Thanks Mandy," Emma said in a joking tone.

Mandy headed downstairs with a pillow and blanket, and Emma headed down the hall to the spare room where she knew Cathy had some extra men's pajamas stashed away in case Liam ever needed them.

"Here," Emma said, her cheeks flushing a little as she handed him the pjs. Reality began sinking in a little now that she was back inside the house and out of the storm. Had she really kissed Michael?

"Thanks," he said, offering her a warm smile back. No signs of regret were in his eyes when she met his.

"I'm going to get some dry clothes on, but it looks like we are all having an old-fashioned sleepover downstairs tonight. I'll see you down there," Emma said, before heading down the hall to her bedroom.

"See you," he said behind her. She heard the bathroom door shut right before closing her bedroom door. Emma leaned against the backside of her door, taking a moment to process while she was still alone.

"Did I really just kiss Michael?" she thought again, trying to catch her mind up with the events that had just occurred.

But she had. And now she had to consider what exactly that meant.

Emma towel dried her hair and slipped into fresh clothes, feeling like a new person after she had.

By the time she reached the basement, Mandy and Michael were both downstairs, laughing as they flipped through movie options, debating like old friends about what they wanted to put on to fall asleep to. Mandy had already set up the pull-out couch bed and Michael had an air mattress blowing up as he made a makeshift bed on the floor.

"If it wasn't so doom and gloom outside and it wasn't almost one in the morning, this could actually be a pretty fun adult sleepover," Mandy said, selecting the movie that she and Michael had finally agreed on.

Emma had to admit, it was nice seeing her best friend and Michael interacting. She knew Mandy well enough to know she already approved of Michael. Although Emma wasn't sure when she should tell her friend about what had just happened outside. She was still processing that herself.

And then there was Liam. It would only be fair to end things the right way with him if she wanted to be with Michael. But did she want to be with Michael, or had she simply explored feelings she was still figuring out herself?

"No need to make any decisions tonight," she thought.

Emma turned off the lights slid next to Mandy on the pull-out couch and Michael sat on his air mattress bed on the floor as the throwback nineties romantic comedy began playing in front of them.

"Goodnight, Mandy, Goodnight Michael," Emma said, looking over and seeing his face dimly lit in the light of the TV. She couldn't make out his expression, but she saw his head turn to look directly at her.

"Goodnight, Emma," Michael said.

"Goodnight, friend," Mandy said, hugging Emma before she rolled over.

Emma was too tired to let her mind wander over the possibility of 'what if' with Michael for long.

Within a matter of minutes, Emma had fallen into a deep sleep.

Chapter Twelve

The day following the storm was a busy one.

Emma didn't mind though; that meant she had more time to let the reality of last night sink in and really consider what that meant for her. Fortunately, Manny's owner had been very understanding and grateful for how she handled his storm anxiety and thanked her for keeping him safe. Apparently, his storm anxiety had been getting worse with age and last night's mega storm must have really put him over the edge.

However, life's timing has a funny way of throwing you curve balls.

The kind that likes to wreak havoc on your emotions. For Emma, that curve ball came in the form of a phone call from the one person she didn't expect to hear from after almost total radio silence: Liam.

Emma saw his name flash across her phone, freezing when it did. For over a week and a half she had had nothing but a short text leading to small talk and nothing since. But lo and behold, here he was, calling her out of the blue as if he sensed the events that occurred last night. To be fair, there had been a pretty nasty storm that ripped through their part of Florida. Perhaps he was simply making sure she, and his aunt's farm, was still standing.

"Hello?" Emma said, answering the phone as she ducked out of the barn aisle, leaning against the wood siding of the barn's far side.

"Hey Em, I was just calling to make sure you and everyone at the farm were doing ok. Aunt Cathy had a brunch with friends this morning but wanted me to call and check in," Liam said.

"*Ah, ok, so this was mainly Cathy's doing,*" Emma thought. Cathy knew all too well how this break relationship limbo was wreaking havoc on her emotions. It made Emma feel slightly less guilty that he was simply calling to make sure they were alive.

"The farm is still standing. We are just doing a lot of clean up since debris ended up all over the farm and we had a couple fence boards that needed repaired. We got lucky," Emma replied as casually as she could.

"Good, I'm glad everyone is safe and there wasn't too much damage. Listen, Em, I know the way I left things wasn't fair to you. I was angry, and I'm still working through that. But I miss you and I hope you know I still care about you. I know we have a lot to work through, but I want to…," Liam said. He was still talking, but Emma's mind was already panicking. Was he really about to ask her to try and work things out? Of course, he had no idea about last night and if he did, that would be the end of that. More importantly, it would hurt him all over again.

"Liam, I think you were right," Emma said, cutting him off mid-sentence.

"Right about what?" Liam asked, sounding confused.

"Right about taking a break to figure things out. I know this started because of what happened between Michael and I a few months ago, but I think there was a bigger problem before you knew about that. I think we need to think about...well, if this relationship is even working. Liam, you live almost four hours away, your job keeps you insanely busy, and my life is here, at this farm with the horses. We just live different lives than we did when we re-connected in Wellington, you know? I just...I just think we need to think about that. I don't think we should get back together," she said, the words coming out unevenly as she tried to relay them.

Tears rolled down her cheek though as she spoke to them. It broke her heart to hurt him, and she had never stopped caring about him. But still, she meant what she said. This had been something she had been struggling with since she moved back to Ocala. Emma may not have had time to consider exactly what she wanted yet, but she had just been confronted with a choice, and in this moment, it felt like the right one.

Liam was quiet on the other side of the phone for a moment before he spoke again.

"If that's how you feel," he said shortly.

"It is," Emma replied, softening her words.

"Well, I'm glad you're ok. I guess I'll talk to you at some point," Liam said.

"Thanks, I'll talk to you...," Emma began, but Liam hung up the phone mid-sentence. Tears came harder now; she hated the fact that she had hurt Liam twice now.

Emma recalled her own feelings after her previous boyfriend, Jordan, had broken up with her what seemed like so long ago now. It killed her that she might now be causing Liam to feel that way.

Pulling herself together, she went back into the barn and slipped a halter over Valentine's head. Her work was done for the day, Michael was out back fixing the last of the fence boards, and Sam had headed home half an hour ago.

"Hey Val," she cooed to the mare, leading her out of her stall with a half clipped on halter and no lead rope; truth be told Valentine probably would have followed her down the aisle to the grooming bay without one. Emma had already planned to ride her horse today, just a light hack around the back side of the property, but now she *needed* to ride. Right this second.

Emma used a soft brush to flick the light dust from her coat before sliding the bit into her mouth and bridle over her head. They headed for the mounting block outside, and Emma slid her leg over her mare's bare back.

They headed down the hill into the cooler area where the trees were scattered around, casting shade over most of this part of the field. The air that was thick and humid yesterday but it had turned into a much cooler, less humid day today. It was a welcomed relief and made for perfect early evening riding weather.

Emma trotted around the field, letting the sun and her horse take away her worries as they rode around carefree. When she reached the edge of the property's border, Emma turned around, facing towards home, a smirk breaking out on her face. It had been a long time since she felt the freedom of galloping bareback on her horse. Come to think of it, she hadn't galloped bareback since that day on the beach when Bo had chased her.

"Well then it's long overdue," she thought.

"Want to go for a little gallop, girl?" Emma asked her mare, whose ears swiveled back as she listened to her owner's voice.

Wrapping both legs around her horse and while simultaneously making a kissing sound, she felt her mare take off immediately. Valentine loved to stretch her legs and needed very little encouragement to move into this forward pace.

They tore across the ground, chunks of grass and mud flying behind them as they galloped full speed across the open pasture. There was something special and exhilarating about galloping bareback. There was nothing between her and her horse as she felt every muscle contract and relax, every hoof touching ground and reaching out underneath her. Nothing in the world compared to this feeling. And there was nothing that made her feel freer and more alive.

Emma laughed as she asked her horse to slow, who reluctantly broke back to a trot and then a walk. To her surprise, Michael stood not too far from where they stopped, hammer still in his hand from where he had fixed a nearby fence board.

"Looks like you guys had a good time," he said, laughing as Valentine tried to break back into a trot again. Her mare clearly would have been happy galloping for a lot longer had Emma let her.

"We did," Emma said, smiling at Michael. She had to admit, looking at him now after talking to Liam and truly ending things made her feel like a weight had been lifted. She still had a lot to process about her new feelings for Michael, like should she even be jumping into any kind of relationship so soon, but at least now there wasn't the guilt that followed when she considered it.

"See you after your ride," Michael said, placing his hand on Valentine's shoulder as he gave her a pat.

"See you," Emma said, locking eyes with him a moment before they walked off.

After walking her horse out, Emma headed back to the barn and put her horse away. Michael was already getting grain ready for evening feed and Emma began throwing hay. They worked together in silence until all the horses had been fed.

Emma closed the feed room door to see Michael leaning against the side the of the barn. There was a moment where neither of them seemed to know what to do next. Normally they both simply said goodnight and went back to their respective homes. But after last night, everything was different.

"Do you and Mandy have dinner plans tonight?" Michael asked.

"Nothing too exciting. We planned to order some take-out and hang out since she is only in town a few more days," Emma said. She was curious now what his motive was behind the question.

"That sounds fun," he said, taking a step closer. "I guess I will see you tomorrow then?"

"Have a good night," Emma said, although she still didn't know exactly what to do next.

Michael took a few more steps closer, pulling her in and wrapping his arms around her waist and kissing her on the cheek. Clearly neither of them was quite sure what was going on between them.

"Goodnight," he said, looking over his shoulder as he headed towards his apartment.

Emma headed back toward the house, her head spinning. Mandy really couldn't have come for a visit at a better time. She still hadn't told Mandy about last night's kiss between her and Michael, but she had every intention of telling her tonight.

To her surprise, she found Mandy out front of the house sitting in a chair with her laptop on her lap.

"I thought you were on vacation," Emma teased.

"Please, you know that means nothing. I'm always working," Mandy said, shutting her laptop. "I'm done for the day though, I promise," she said, putting her hands up.

"Good, because I have some things to tell you and you're not going to want to miss this," Emma said, pulling up a chair next to her friend.

Mandy put her laptop away, leaning in closer to her friend, ready to hear whatever juicy bit of information Emma was about to tell her.

"I kissed Michael last night, on the front porch, after we ran back to the house through the storm," Emma blurted out.

"What! Tell me everything," Mandy said, scooting her chair even closer now, eyes wide.

Emma told her best friend every detail about last night and then her call with Liam earlier that day. Mandy listened intently, hanging on every word, asking questions now and then.

She had to admit, it felt like old times. Back when they were roommates, they told each other everything; they were like sisters. It couldn't be better timing for something like this to happen. Sure, she would have called Mandy and told her everything anyway, but having her right here in person? Well, it made it that much better.

"So now I guess I'm just trying to figure out what the next step is. I just don't know that I should jump right into anything with Michael though, you know? We work together every day, and Liam and I just broke up," Emma said.

"Take it slow then. I'm sure you will figure it out as you go," Mandy said, squeezing her friend's hand.

Emma smiled at Mandy and leaned back into her chair, taking a deep breath as she looked out over the gorgeous property in front of them.

Truly, she had so much to be thankful for. Things seemed like were only going to go up from here.

Emma pointed the hose at Piper's face, laughing as the mare lipped at the hose water. She had never met a horse who loved bath time more than sweet Piper. Normally this mare wasn't on her schedule to ride, but Piper's owner was on vacation and asked Emma to work the horse while she was away. Emma happily agreed; she was a super fancy horse with excellent training and one of those easy and enjoyable rides.

"Ok missy, I think bath time is over. You've wasted half of the water in Ocala," Emma said, turning off the hose. Piper side-eyed her, stretching her head and neck out to sniff the now limp hose as she put it back on the stand. Clearly, she was not happy her bath time was over.

Emma squeegeed the water off her chestnut coat and put her back in her stall. She thought about her and Mandy's conversation last night, and while she and Michael had been going about business-as-usual today, Emma planned to talk to him after work tonight. She was sure he would understand her wanting to take things slow and keep whatever was between them on the down low for now, given the circumstances.

Hanging the halter on Piper's stall, Emma walked towards the feed room, ready to begin her nightly routine.

Before she could make it that far though, something stopped Emma in her tracks. It would be a sound that would forever remind her of this very moment. It was the sound of truck tires peeling out, fighting to gain traction on the concrete.

"What was that?" Emma thought. It didn't quite sound like the truck was in the driveway. Maybe somewhere outside on the back road next to the farm?

Emma was about to disregard the sound, but she heard someone yell a loud, "Hey!" followed by another truck's engine firing up and peeling out, pausing briefly as it waited for the metal gates at the entrance. The truck fought for traction again as the driver punched the gas, burning out before it blasted down the road.

"What is going on?!" Emma thought, jogging out of the barn as she squinted her eyes, trying to see if she could make out anything in the distance. Whoever it was had to be too far down the road now.

But she quickly noticed Sam's truck was gone. What had he seen, and why had he left in such a hurry?

The image of Michael running from where he had been across property on the lawn, caught her attention out of the corner of her eye. He didn't stop until he had reached her.

He placed one hand on her arm, looking at her with a worried expression.

"I heard tires squealing and saw Sam peeling out. What happened?" he asked, his eyes scanning the property for anything else that might be amiss.

"I heard him yelling at someone or something before he peeled out. I don't know what's happening," she said. An eerie feeling was beginning to wash over her though. Something wasn't right, and she could feel it.

"Is Mandy still up at the house? Maybe she saw something out of the house windows?"

Emma glanced at where her car was still parked in the front of the property.

"Her car is still here. Let's go see what she knows," Emma said, wasting no time as she began jogging toward the house with Michael right behind her. She noticed Mandy's laptop sitting on the patio table outside, her phone sitting next to it.

"Mandy!" Emma called out, opening the front door to the house. Maybe she was in the bathroom? Or the spare bedroom? Michael waited in the living room as Emma opened the door to both the bedroom and bathroom but no Mandy.

"She's not in here," Emma said, returning to where Michael stood. Emma racked her brain, trying to think of where her friend could be.

"Maybe she's downstairs for some reason? Napping?" Michael suggested. Emma nodded and headed downstairs. Still no Mandy. That was when a feeling of panic began to wash over her. It started in her toes and seemed to rise up through her whole body. The truck peeling out, Sam, who would never just up and leave work, following whoever that was.

Before the panic completely overwhelmed her, she heard truck tires on the concrete again, this time coming back into the farm.

"Sam's back," she thought. Emma and Michael exchanged a quick worried glance as they ran outside where Sam was already clambering out of his truck, running in their direction.

"Sam, what's happening?" Emma asked, her voice sounded oddly calm. Was this the beginning of shock?

Sam's eyes darted from her face to Michael's, a look of panic reflected in his eyes as well.

"Someone took Mandy," Sam said, his voice sounding bewildered.

"What?! How?!" Emma asked, feeling dizzy now.

"I'm not sure. I was working on cutting back some weeds over on the fence line and I saw this guy carrying Mandy. He climbed through the fence at the front of the property. He pulled her over the fence. She looked knocked out, maybe he drugged her or something? I don't know. I yelled at him after I saw him, but he peeled out quickly. I tried to chase him down, but he was too far ahead of me, and I lost him. I'm so sorry, Emma, I tried," Sam said, his eyes conveying his sympathy.

"She's gone?" Emma said, more as a statement, trying to wrap her head around it all. Why would someone do this? It just didn't make any sense.

"Did she have her phone in her pocket or something? Maybe we can track her phone?" Sam suggested.

"No, I think I saw it by her computer over here," Emma said, pointing as she walked over to where Mandy had been working. Emma picked up her friend's phone, knowing it didn't have password protection. She remembered Mandy saying she shut off the password protection when she got this job because it drove her nuts having to type it in every time she got a call or message, which was all the time, and only slowed her down.

Emma unlocked the screen and gasped out loud when she saw the text message from a restricted number in front of her.

Michael looked over at her, his face scrunched with concern.

Emma reread the message, then read it again. She fought the urge to throw up as she handed the phone to Michael. There was no way she could read the message aloud without losing it.

"What does it say?" Sam asked, watching Michael's expression change as he read the text for himself. Michael cleared his throat, seeming to gather himself before reading it aloud. He shot a look at Emma; he seemed concerned about what it might do to her to say the words out loud.

"It says: *You have twenty-four hours to deposit $30,000 into this account if you ever want to see your friend again. No cops.* Then it lists the account number and bank," Michael said, shooting another look at Emma, whose complexion looked snow white now.

"We need to call Cathy," Emma mumbled, pulling her own phone from her pocket. Her hand trembled, and the dizziness seemed to be intensifying by the second. Before she knew what was happening, her ears were ringing and the world seemed to close in around her, fading her vision to black.

"Em? Emma?" A voice said, sounding like it was at the other end of a long hallway. "I think she passed out," the voice said, sounding a little closer now.

"Michael?" she said, identifying the voice now as she opened her eyes. She was slumped in the chair near where she had been standing, no doubt where Michael had placed her after she passed out.

"Cathy. We need to call Cathy," Emma mumbled.

"He's on the phone with her now," Sam said, who was standing next to the chair.

"She's ok, Cathy, I think she's just a little overwhelmed. Yes, that's what the text said. I'm sorry, I know this is a lot to ask. Yes, I will tell Emma. Ok, thanks again," Michael said before hanging up the phone.

Emma was sitting up now, her head still feeling fuzzy. However, she needed to know what was going on.

"What did she say?" Emma asked, staring intently at Michael who had just hung up the phone. Emma tried to push herself out of the chair.

"Cathy's depositing the money into the account now. She fought me at first on the no cops thing, but in the end she agreed to keep them out of it for now, given the circumstance. Cathy also told me to make sure you take it easy and keep her posted," Michael replied, helping Emma, who almost fell trying to get out of the chair. "We need to get you inside though. Maybe you should lie down for a while?" Michael added, concern written all over his face.

"How am I supposed to sleep knowing my best friend is missing?! I wish there was something I could do," Emma said, fighting back tears now.

"Cathy seems to have it handled; I'm sure everything will be fine," Sam said, trying to reassure her as well.

Despite her protests, Michael all but carried her into the house, setting her down on the couch.

"I need to feed the horses," Emma said, although her head still spun.

"I've got it," Sam said, heading out the front door before Emma could protest.

"Thank you," Michael called after him.

"Try to rest. I have the phone right here in case anything happens. I'll be right here too," Michael said in a soft, reassuring tone. He picked the remote off of the coffee table and turned on the TV, flipping through the channels until he found something he thought she might like.

"Thanks," Emma croaked, her throat feeling dry and hoarse. Before she could ask for water, she felt the dizziness take over. It was as if the intense wave of emotions that overtook her when she found out her friend was missing had drained every ounce of energy in her body. Her eyes felt heavy and before she knew it, she had dozed off. The last thing she remembered thinking was that she was just going to rest her eyes for a little bit, and then she would be refreshed enough to stay up the rest of the night in case there was any news on Mandy's return.

But Emma's body had other plans, and she slept soundly until dawn the next day.

Chapter Thirteen

Emma's eyes flew open, taking in the early morning light as reality set in.

"No!" she thought. Michael was still slumped in the recliner next to the couch, passed out.

Emma scrambled to get up, grabbing her phone first as she looked to see if she had any missed calls or messages.

"Nothing?!" she thought, grabbing Michael's phone next, which also had no missed calls or messages.

"Michael!" Emma said, and his head flew up, looking around as he got his bearings.

"What's happening?" he asked, still processing that it was morning too.

"Nothing apparently. Neither of us have any missed calls or messages. Did you hear anything last night before you went to sleep?" she asked, desperate to know if the money transfer had worked. But if it had, why hadn't they heard anything? And why hadn't Mandy been returned? In this case, no news *wasn't* good news.

"No, nothing. I fell asleep late, maybe midnight, but no one reached out before I passed out," Michael replied.

"Where's Mandy's phone?" Emma asked, desperation creeping into her voice now.

"Kitchen counter," Michael said, pointing in its direction.

Emma stood up quickly, power walking to the counter. Mandy's phone had a couple calls and texts from co-workers and her boss, but nothing from the restricted number. Nothing about her kidnapping.

Emma used the counter to keep herself steady as she processed that news. She was sure Cathy had deposited the money like she said. So why hadn't they heard anything?

Emma all but ran back to her phone and called Cathy.

"Cathy?"

"Emma, dear! Is Mandy back yet?" Cathy asked, interrupting her. Emma's heart sank.

"That's actually why I'm calling. Did the money deposit go through ok?" she replied.

"Yes, of course," Cathy said, sounding concerned now too.

"I can't tell you how much I appreciate you doing this. I hope we hear from her soon. I'll keep you posted, ok?"

"Alright dear, try not to worry too much," Cathy said.

Emma slumped back into the couch cushions, rubbing her temples with her fingertips, fighting the now all too familiar feeling of nausea in her gut. Michael sat down next to her, wrapping his arm around her shoulders as he pulled her close.

"I'm sure she'll be back soon," Michael said, rubbing her arm as he kissed her forehead.

"I'm going to go feed the horses breakfast," she said, getting up. If she sat here any longer, she was going to lose her mind.

"I'll help you," Michael said. Emma didn't protest. Without Michael at her side, she would have lost it a long time ago.

She mindlessly went through her morning routine as she tossed flakes of hay and poured grain into horses' buckets. Still, her mind wandered to where her best friend might be. Was she scared? Was she injured? *Where* was she? And the biggest question of all was *why*? Why her?

Her head swam with endless, unanswered questions.

Her phone buzzed in her pocket, making her jump. She whipped it out, locking her eyes onto the screen in a desperate hope for good news. Lily's name and picture flashed across the screen. Did she know their friend was missing?

"Lil?"

"Emma, I think there's something you should know," Lily said on the other end of the phone.

"Ok but first, I have some bad news, Lily," Emma replied.

"So do I. Wait, what's your news?" Lily said, sounding confused.

"Mandy was kidnapped yesterday. We don't know why or where she is, but whoever took her sent a text to her phone saying to pay them $30,000 into a checking account. Cathy paid it, but we haven't heard from Mandy yet, and I'm starting to get really worried. I think I may have to call the police soon, but they said no cops so I'm not sure if I should...," Emma said, but Lily cut her off before she could finish.

"Em, I think I know who took her."

"Who?!" Emma asked.

"Clint." Lily said, sounding quite sure.

"Clint, as in Clint who works at Three Phases Farm? Why would he take Mandy? He doesn't even know her," Emma said.

"Because Clint is Bo's brother," Lily stated.

"Bo's brother? As in the Bo who stalked me?" she thought.

"Wait, how do you know?" Emma replied.

"Well, Clint didn't show up for work for a week straight without warning, and he never returned any of our calls or texts. Recently, calls just started going straight to voicemail so we assumed he decided to quit without telling us. So, we sent a cleaning crew in to clean out his living quarters, and they found an envelope hidden under his mattress. It contained a letter Bo sent his brother from jail and the last paycheck he got from High Pointe Stables. I guess he sent money back home to his family regularly. It doesn't give us a ton of details, but I think Bo's family depended on that money because in his letter, Bo is apologizing for what he did and that he knows this means they could lose the house without his financial support," Lily replied.

Emma remembered back to when she worked at Three Phases Farm. She recalled the day she had handed off a horse to be untacked, and the way Clint had glared at her with such resentment. She had assumed at the time he was upset about her not untacking the horse she rode, but now, it all made sense. His anger had been about what he blamed Emma for: locking up his brother in prison, and consequently, cutting off the funds his family back home so desperately needed. If Emma knew one thing it is that money, or lack thereof, and family ties drove people to do some crazy things. Crazy things like kidnapping the best friend of the person he thought was responsible for his problems.

"Oh my gosh," Emma said into the phone, as the pieces fell into place. Still, this changed nothing about the situation. If they called the cops, Mandy may never come home. If they didn't, would she still come home? They had given him what they wanted, hadn't they? He had the money well before the twenty-four hour mark.

"Em, why hasn't Mandy come back yet if he has the money?" Lily asked, her voice exposing her own panic now.

"I don't...I don't know," Emma stammered. There had to be a reason Clint hadn't brought Mandy home. There were two possibilities as to why, but her mind wasn't ready to explore the second. Emma shuttered, afraid to even go there.

Michael stood a few feet from her, his eyes locked onto her face, reading her expressions as she talked to Lily. Suddenly, Emma realized she had left Mandy's phone on the counter. If her theory about the first possibility was right, she needed to check it right away.

"Lil, I've got to go, but I'll keep you posted," Emma said.

"Ok, thanks Em," Lily said, her voice sounding shaken now.

Emma said nothing to Michael but spun on her heels and ran full sprint back to the house. She burst through the front door, grabbing the phone where it still lay on the kitchen counter.

Emma unlocked the screen, scrolling past more missed calls and messages from work. She felt a little bad about not at least alerting Mandy's boss about what was going on, but right now she was focused on one thing: finding her best friend.

Her finger stopped scrolling as her eyes locked on a new message from a restricted number just as Michael was opening the door behind her. Instantly, she felt a wave of relief that she had some news on her friend, but it was quickly replaced by what felt like someone punching her in the gut as she skimmed the preview part of the message visible on the screen. Clicking on the message in its entirety, Emma prepared to read it aloud as Michael put a hand on her back, clearly steadying her in case she passed out again.

"I need more money. Deposit $500,000 dollars into the same account within twenty-four hours or you will never see her again. No cops," Emma read, yesterday's dizziness threatening her balance again. Emma took a deep breath, closing her eyes a moment, holding onto the feeling of Michael's hand on her back, grounding herself to it.

Emma turned the phone so Michael could see the picture attached to the message. His eyes scanned the picture of Mandy tied to a chair in front of a cabin. Wherever she was looked like it was in a heavily wooded area.

"Does Cathy have that kind of money?" Michael asked.

"Cathy may be loaded, but I don't know that she has that much cash lying around after she just purchased this farm," Emma replied. She fought the darkness threating to overwhelm her again. Emma did not have time to pass out. She had to save her friend.

Taking slow, deep breaths again as her chest tightened, Emma called Cathy, although, she had a sinking feeling she knew how this call was going to go. She briefed Cathy on the most recent message from the kidnapper.

"Oh honey," Cathy said, audibly gasping on the other end. "You know I would do anything to get Mandy back, but I don't have that kind of liquid cash. Most of that went into the down payment of the farm. We would have to sell it to get that kind of cash, and we still wouldn't be able to get it in time. I will reach out to some friends, see if I can get some people to pitch in, but that is a very short amount of time to get that kind of cash," Cathy replied, confirming her fears.

"I understand, thanks for everything Cathy," Emma said, defeat clear in her voice now.

"I'll do everything I can, dear. I'll keep you posted," Cathy replied.

Emma thanked her once more before hanging up the phone. She leaned against Michael, feeling weak and defeated. Now what? She couldn't simply wait around hoping Cathy could find enough wealthy friends willing to give her half a million dollars in less than a day. There had to be something she could do to find her friend herself.

Emma ran through the facts in her mind. Clint didn't own any property here, and he was at some sort of cabin, probably not far from here since the bank account led back to a local Ocala bank, one that didn't have branches anywhere else. If he wanted to cash out all the money, he had to stay local. Why had he done that? There had to be a reason.

Either way, it narrowed her search down to Ocala and the surrounding areas. He didn't own property, so he would have had to rent a cabin. And based on his current financial situation, it had to be something cheap. Clint was normally not a criminal, and he had sent a picture with far too much of the cabin pictured, making it fairly identifiable if she could find the one he had rented.

Emma suddenly caught a second wind and headed down the hallway to her bedroom where her laptop was. She opened it, clicking on the first search engine icon she saw and typed in 'cabins for rent in Ocala.' Filtering out the more expensive ones and ones that were in locations that would be too public for hiding a kidnapped woman, she began scrolling down the first page, looking for any pictures that reminded her of the cabin she saw in the picture Clint sent.

Michael peeked around the corner of her bedroom door, a worried look on his face. He probably thought she was losing her mind. Maybe she was.

"I'm looking for the cabin Clint rented. He's holding her hostage somewhere close; I know it," she said, not looking up from her search as she spoke.

Michael sat next to her on the bed, pulling out his phone.

"Tell me what to search. I'll help," he said. Emma briefed him on her theory and Michael got to work, searching through the list of cabins another site populated based on their specific filters.

Emma's eyes felt dry and were surely red as she closed them for a moment. How long had they been looking through cabins now? Two hours? Three?

At some point Sam had stopped by the house, checking in with them, and they shared with him the bleak update from that morning. He told them not to worry about anything in the barn and that he would make sure the horses were taken care of. Emma peeled herself away from the computer long enough to call a couple of the owners of the horses she was scheduled to work today and explain why she would need at least a couple days off. Luckily, they were all more than understanding. Clara in particular even offered to help work some of those horses for a few days while Emma was off. While she hated taking any more time away from her search than necessary, Emma also made a call to Mandy's boss. She told herself that Mandy would still want to have a job when she came home.

When, she came home, not *if*. Emma was determined to find her best friend if it was the last thing she did. After that, hours passed by in lurches, as they went through site after site of cabin rentals, sometimes twice to make sure they didn't miss anything, changing search filter settings multiple times.

Emma's stomach rumbled, but she ignored it. Michael shot her a look from across the living room where they were now sitting.

"We should probably make some dinner," he said cautiously, knowing she had to be hungry but also knowing she was probably too stubborn to stop searching until she found a cabin that looked like the one where Mandy was being held hostage. The way Michael looked at her, Emma wondered if he was losing hope.

Not that she blamed him; after all, this plan was a little bit of a long shot. Still, Emma would never be able to forgive herself if she didn't do everything in her power to try and help find Mandy.

"I'm ok," Emma replied, barely glancing up from her laptop. Michael stood up and walked over to where she sat, resting a hand on her shoulder.

"Em, I'm going to make you something to eat. You can't help Mandy if you pass out from starvation," he said, adding a little bit of a teasing tone to his voice in hopes of lightening her mood. It was sweet he was trying to take care of her.

"Ok, I guess...thanks," Emma said, looking up him with a grateful smile. What would she have done without him here during all of this?

Michael found a frozen pizza and pre-heated the oven. By the time the pizza was halfway cooked, Emma realized just how ravenous she was. She had skipped lunch and had hardly eaten breakfast. Really, she was running on fumes.

Emma took a bite of the now cooked pizza as she opened up a website she had already searched through twice now. Sighing, she changed the search engine filters once more; she had to be sure before she crossed it off the list. Changing the price point and pushing the distance radius a little further out, she scanned through the search results, passing over many she had already seen and confirmed were not Clint's cabin.

Emma froze, scrolling back as her eyes suddenly widened. She set the half piece of pizza down as she locked her focus in on the cabin in the picture, zooming into the exterior photo as she scanned the color and design. Pulling Mandy's phone frantically from where it rested on the coffee table, she compared the two images.

"Michael!" she shouted, her voice a mix of stunned and excited. Was this it? Michael quickly walked over, and Emma handed him the laptop as she grabbed her phone from where it lay next to her on the couch.

Dialing Lily's number, she waited impatiently for her friend to answer.

"Lily? Are you at Three Phases Farm right now?" Emma asked quickly.

"Yes, what's going on?" Lily replied.

"Good! Ok, I need you to do me a favor. Can you check that storage pole barn with all the extra farm equipment and see if there is a four-wheeler missing?" Emma said.

"On it," Lily said.

Emma waited as her friend sprinted across the field towards the pole barn. She could hear the wind whooshing across the phone as she ran, thankful Lily had caught on quickly to what she was getting at and understood the urgency of the question.

"It looks like we are missing a four-wheeler!" Lily said breathlessly.

"It does?! Ok good. Lil, I think we found the cabin he has Mandy. It's in a really remote spot; the description says you can only get back there by four-wheeler or horseback. It's one of those super secluded ones in the middle of the Ocala National Forest. This thing doesn't even have power; it looks like it's ancient!" Emma said.

"Be careful, whatever you do, and keep me posted," Lily replied on the other line.

"I promise to keep you posted. Thanks Lily!" Emma said, hanging up the phone.

Emma turned back toward Michael, whose head was cocked with curiosity as he listened to one half of their conversation.

"Em, I think you're right. It looks just like the picture. Maybe we should call the police," Michael began.

"Michael, if he catches wind of the police coming, what then? He could...he...," Emma choked up, the words getting caught in her throat. She couldn't even say them.

"We have to save her ourselves," Emma managed to finally spit out.

Michael took a deep breath, clearly considering what he was about to get himself into. But one more look at Emma and his expression softened.

"Ok, Em. Let's go get Mandy," Michael said, looking like he might be regretting his own words even as he spoke them.

Emma and Michael spent the next ten minutes formulating a plan.

Since they didn't have a four-wheeler at Live Oaks Farm yet, horseback would be their only option into the deep part of the forest where the cabin lay. Emma would ride Valentine, and Michael would take Manny since he was retired from competing and an easy ride. Luckily, when Emma had made a call to his owner, she had agreed to let them borrow him, given the circumstances. She promised his owners to take good care of him. Emma wasn't thrilled about putting Valentine or Manny in any kind of danger, but she planned to tie them up nearby once they got close to the cabin. Not that she expected Michael to let her get anywhere near it once they discovered it anyway.

Michael tried to talk her out of coming together, saying he would bring Sam with him instead. Of course, Emma shot down that idea quickly; no way she was sitting at home wondering what was going on. Her best friend needed her, and she was going to help find her. Besides, she felt responsible for her being in this situation in the first place.

Michael pulled the truck and horse trailer around so Emma could start packing what they needed for the horses. Michael excused himself after loading up Manny, saying he needed to grab a few things from his apartment. Emma didn't ask questions; she knew whatever he was getting was for their own protection. She hated the idea of putting Michael in danger too, but she also knew he could take care of himself. Plus, Clint was no normal criminal, at least until recently, she reminded himself. He was a desperate man who did a stupid, desperate thing to try and get money. She hoped once they caught him, he would simply surrender. Or run. If he ran, then what? Did they chase him? Let him go?

Emma shook her head, clearing her thoughts.

"One thing at a time," she thought.

Emma wrapped both horses' legs in polo wraps so they would be safe from any thick brush in the forest and grabbed the saddle bag so she could bring some food and water.

Michael returned with flashlights, and a few other necessities in case it got dark before they got to the cabin. Right now, they only had a few hours left of daylight. She hoped that was enough.

The problem with the limited information they had about the cabin on the website was that the address was only made available after someone booked it. However, Michael, the ex-boy scout he was, had pulled out a map and pinpointed the location pretty closely with his phone's GPS. That would get them close enough, and from there, they would just have to search until they found the cabin.

It made Emma sick to think they had discovered the cabin so late in the day. Being so close to dusk was not ideal, but at least they had a lead. Not to mention the clock was ticking; by mid-morning tomorrow the twenty-four hours they had to deposit half a million dollars would be over. Cathy had called her a few hours ago saying she had managed to get a promise of funds from a couple friends, but that she still needed over half of the amount Clint had requested. Emma shuttered thinking about that.

With her horse also now in the trailer and everything packed up, Emma peeked into the barn where Sam was throwing hay to the horses.

"Hey, thanks for taking care of everything for us while we are away," Emma said to Sam.

"Of course. Y'all go get your girl!" Sam said, his southern accent coming out a little more than usual. Emma smiled for the first time in well over a day and jogged over to the passenger side of the truck, hopping in quickly.

"Let's go!" she said, turning to Michael. He looked back over at her as he put the truck in gear, worry and determination mixed in those green eyes staring back. Worry she knew, that was directed at her.

"I'll be fine," Emma said, answering his unspoken question. "Valentine has my back and so do you," she added, shooting him a reassuring smile.

Michael drove as quickly as safety would allow as they tore down route twenty-seven and they made their way toward the Ocala National Forest. Emma watched as live oaks and palm trees resting on rolling hills blurred by with the sun peeking in and out from behind them as it began its slow decent. Her heart pounded just thinking about what they were about to do.

"Ocala National Forest" the sign read, as they entered into a deeply wooded area. Not even a mile in and they passed a 'bear crossing' sign.

"That's promising," she thought sarcastically.

Michael parked in the closest public parking area to the cabins he could. Emma pulled her horse off the trailer, and Valentine's ears swiveled around as she took in the lush tropical forest around them. Valentine didn't seem fazed, and neither did Manny, who was more interested in eating the grass below him than anything else.

They tacked up the horses and Michael stuffed their supplies into his backpack, putting it on before he mounted up.

"Sorry, Em, I know this isn't exactly an ideal first horseback ride together, is it?" Michael said, as Emma swung her leg over her own horse's back.

Emma looked over at Michael, essentially her hero of the day. Who else would go traipsing around a seven-hundred-mile wilderness looking for a missing person? No doubt about it; he was truly a good man.

"Don't worry, I'm sure this isn't the last time," she teased. Trouble did seem to follow her, after all.

Michael pulled out his map and set his GPS as they headed into the tall pines. Really, the forest was breathtaking. Under normal circumstances, this would have been a relaxing ride through some of the wildest and most beautiful tropical forest she had ever seen. Emma had always wanted to ride through here, just not while looking for her kidnapped best friend.

They rode along at a walk or trot for almost a mile, mostly in silence, as they took in the rich tropical foliage, tall pines, oak trees, and the occasional palm tree. It was too heavily wooded to go much faster. Valentine looked around, plodding along happily as if they were on a fun leisurely trail ride with no ulterior mission. Manny also seemed to be enjoying himself and was being a very good boy for his rider. Emma couldn't help but sneak a glance now and then to watch Michael on horseback for the first time. Despite never seeing him ride before now, he looked like a natural. Of course, he had spent plenty of time in the saddle growing up thanks to his grandfather. Still, it had been several years since he had ridden from what he told her.

"So, before everything happened yesterday, I planned on talking to you about that kiss," Emma said, suddenly breaking the silence.

"What about it?" Michael asked, turning his head in her direction, one eyebrow raised curiously.

"Well, what it means for us, I guess," Emma said awkwardly.

Michael paused, seeming to think on her words for a moment.

"What do you want it to mean?" he asked softly.

"I want to explore whatever this is between us. But...," she began, cutting herself off to think a moment.

"But?"

"*But* I want to take things slow. You know, keep our relationship on the down low and not rush into anything," she said, scanning his expression as she spoke.

Michael paused again, processing.

"I understand. I'm sure you want to talk to Liam and end things with him the right way too." Michael finally said.

"Well, actually I already did. We talked on the phone the other day, and when he started talking about working things out...," Emma began.

"He wanted to get back together?" Michael asked, cutting in, his tone full of surprise.

"Yeah, but I turned him down. I told him we had had other issues before what happened between you and I came out and that it just wasn't a good idea for us to get back together. He wasn't super happy about that, but I think it was the right choice. We are just living different lives than we did when we first started dating," Emma replied.

"That makes sense," Michael said, looking away from her a moment as his eyes drifted back to the forest in front of them. Emma wondered what he was thinking about or what else she should say next.

They walked along in silence for another few minutes. Emma wanted to mention the picture of Jane in his living room or say that it was a small part of the reason she wanted to take things slow because she still wondered if he held onto feelings for her. Feelings that could keep a wall between them. But was she making a bigger deal about that than it needed to be?

"Emma, I've always cared about you," Michael said, finally breaking the silence. Had he read her mind?

"I knew there was something special about you. Something that I was drawn to from the first day you started at Twin Oaks. The closer we became, the more that intensified. One day, I realized it wasn't just friendship I felt for you. It was more than that. I fought it for a long time, and I planned on telling you how I felt when we first got to Wellington...," Michael began.

"...but then I ran into Liam," Emma added, finishing his sentence.

That first week in Wellington came flooding back. The suspicions she had about Michael's romantic feelings for her. The way he touched her hand in that Mexican restaurant when she talked about her plans of whether or not to stay in Florida. She had been right all along. And then she and Liam reconnected, and of course, that blinded her to whatever could have been between her and Michael at that time. Sure, Emma was still hesitant to pursue anything with Michael since they were co-workers, and her internship going well was her top priority. It was the key to her success in her future career, and that meant everything to her. But still, she had wondered about his feelings for her. Back then though, she had never let herself consider that as an option.

"You seemed to really like Liam, and I could tell he liked you. Can't say I blame the guy; he has good taste," Michael added, chuckling a little. "He was the kind of guy you deserved. He could give you everything you wanted, you know? Financial security, his aunt being into horses. Heck, had you not met Cathy you wouldn't be running Live Oaks Farm. Anyway, I decided to back down and let you be happy with him. But that night at the Million Dollar Grand Prix party when I had probably a little too much to drink, I remember thinking how you would be gone soon, out of my life forever. I assumed you would move on to a bigger and better farm, marry Liam, and live a wonderful life. A life you certainly deserved. So, I selfishly let my feelings get the best of me in a moment of weakness, and I kissed you. I'm still sorry I did that though. It wasn't right, and it put you in a position I should have never put you in. I hope you can forgive me for that," Michael said, remorse written all over his face.

"Of course, I forgive you," Emma said, meeting his gaze. Now she knew everything. All the things she had been wondering about. How Michael felt and what went on in his head this past year. Perhaps she should be honest about that picture too?

"As long as we are confessing things, I think I should tell you I saw that picture of Jane sitting on your TV stand in your apartment. I didn't mean to be snooping, I just went in to grab a bottle of water, but it made me think. I wondered if you still held onto feelings for her? Of course, I know you'll always remember her, and she was your fiancé, you have every right to. I guess I just want to know; is it going to hinder you from moving on with me?" Emma asked, her gaze still locked into his.

Michael stared at her, those sparkling green eyes not giving anything away. What was he thinking?

"I feel guilty, Emma. I feel guilty that when I'm with you I forget about Jane. When I'm alone, I think about her sometimes, and miss her, of course. But you changed everything. You made me want to start living again, want to move on. For that, I feel guilty. It's like I'm somehow tarnishing her memory. So I keep her picture out to remind myself that she existed, and so I don't feel like I'm forgetting her. I know it's silly, and I know if she could talk to me right now, she would be happy to know that I was happy and moving on. But that's why it's there; so I don't feel guilty about forgetting her." Michael said, dropping his gaze to the ground.

Poor Michael. She had truly misjudged him once again.

"I didn't know you felt that way. I'm sorry Michael, I didn't mean to question you about her...," Emma started.

"It's ok, Em, really. I get why you were concerned. Just know, it's you, Emma. It's been you for a long time," Michael said, looking back up at her now.

This would have been an excellent time to kiss Michael. Of course, them both being on horseback and on a rescue mission meant that wasn't an option right this second.

Before Emma could answer, the thick forest gave way to a large, open prairie.

"Want to make up some time?" Michael asked, a smirk crossing his face as he looked her way. Emma's mind circled back to the reason they were out here in the first place.

"Definitely," she replied.

Michael looked down at his phone, compass, and then his paper map, making notes on it. They had stopped at the entrance of the park on their way in to pick up one that showed a more zoomed in version of the forest, which Michael had said was a game changer. He had also mentioned he wasn't sure if at some point they were going to lose service and wanted to keep track of where they were going.

"Ok, so we need to start heading west once we cross this clearing, which is that way," he said, pointing to where they would need to go.

"I'll have you know, Valentine waits for no one once we start galloping," Emma said, tossing him a look of warning.

"Well then, it's a good thing I can keep up, now isn't it?" Michael said, a mischievous look crossing his face.

"Ok, don't say I didn't warn you! You are riding an ex-eventing horse, you know," Emma teased, but she still meant it as a warning.

Michael said nothing but asked Manny to canter, which quickly turned into a gallop. Emma watched for half a second, knowing Valentine would easily catch up. Mostly, she wanted to make sure Michael wasn't going to fall off. To her surprise, he appeared fairly well balanced in the saddle. Perhaps he was a better rider than he originally led on?

"Let's go girl," Emma said, legging on Valentine who had been dancing underneath of her since the moment Manny cantered away. Valentine shot off like a rocket, eating up the ground as she closed the gap between them and Manny and Michael. It wasn't long before she was passing them, and Manny picked up his pace, his ears pricked as he followed closely behind her mare. Manny may be retired from eventing, but he was still sound and clearly enjoying his day off the farm.

Emma gave a low whoa to Valentine, pulling her up as they quickly approached the wall of trees in front of them. Manny followed suit, and they both walked into the thick forest in front of them. This part of the forest seemed different though. It was denser with more of the tropical foliage than before. It almost seemed darker too. Or maybe that was because the sun was setting.

"How close are we?" Emma asked, starting to get anxious about finding Mandy.

"We still have a few miles before we get into the radius where the cabin could be. At that point, I don't know how long it will take to cover the wooded area in that radius. Em, I know you don't want to hear this, but it will be dark soon. We may not have a choice but to camp out until morning," Michael said.

"But we only have until morning," Emma said, panic leaking into her voice now.

"I think the cutoff was mid-morning. Don't worry, even if we do camp, we can get up at first light and start looking again. But we have to set up camp before it's too dark, or it will make it twice as hard to do so," he warned.

Emma hoped it wouldn't come to that, but at the rate the forest seemed to be darkening, it wasn't looking good.

Michael continued to lead the way as they walked and trotted through this denser part of the forest. Emma found a few spots where they could canter on and off a few strides, but it was not as much as she would have liked. They stopped anytime they found a clean, clear body of water, letting the horses take long drinks and pulling out their water bottles to hydrate themselves.

"Good news and bad news, Em. We are close, just outside the radius for where this cabin should be located, but if we don't stop and make camp now, it will be way too dark," Michael said, shooting a worried look her way. He knew she wouldn't love hearing they had to stop when they were so close.

"We get up at first light?" Emma asked.

"First light, I promise," Michael said, sliding off Manny's back.

Emma slid off Valentine and pulled tack off of both horses. She had packed their halters and lead ropes in the backpack and found a good place to tie them both. Emma hadn't expected Michael to have room in his backpack for a tent, but to her surprise he had a small, pop up packed in there. Other than two small throw blankets and one of those tiny travel pillows, it looked like they would definitely be roughing it.

Emma remembered tent camping with her family every summer. Sure, they had air mattresses and quite a few other things that made camping a little less rugged than this, but she knew she could survive sleeping one night in the middle of nowhere if it meant she had a shot at saving her best friend. Sleeping on the hard ground was the least of her concerns at this point.

Michael pitched the tent in what felt like no time at all. Emma was glad the horses had already eaten dinner, especially since they weren't going home tonight. While Michael finished setting up and building a small fire, Emma led the horses to an area with grass a few feet away, letting them hand graze while she could. They happily snatched up mouthfuls of grass, immune to the real reason they were on this little expedition.

Emma leaned against her horse's body, resting her head against her soft neck. She couldn't be more thankful for this horse. After all, she had saved her life. Now, maybe Valentine could help her save Mandy's too.

After tying the horses up, Emma sat on the ground next to Michael as he prodded at the fire.

"I guess your boy scout years are paying off, huh?" she asked, still impressed by how quickly he had made camp.

"I'll have to thank my grandpa for forcing me into it as a kid," Michael said, laughing. "Although, once I got into it, I loved it," he added.

They listened to the crackle of the fire for a while, and Emma found her eyes beginning to close without her realizing it.

"Why don't you go to bed, Em? We need our rest for tomorrow anyway," Michael said. He had obviously caught her nodding off.

"Good idea," she said, slowly standing up.

"Are you coming?" she asked.

"No, I'll sleep next to the fire. I'm a southern gentleman, remember?" he said, offering a quick, goofy half smile as he stood up. "Plus, I want to keep an eye on the horses out here," he added. She couldn't argue with that logic.

"Well then, I guess this is goodnight," Emma said, moving into his personal space.

Emma leaned in, ducking around his ball cap as her lips met his. Michael pulled her close, and it felt a little like someone lit a match in her soul.

It felt different this time. The first time they kissed, well, that had been more of a shock than anything. The second time had been like a scene from a movie. Although, it was also a little out of the blue and she hadn't felt quite in her right mind because of the storm and sleep deprivation and all that.

This time, they were in the middle of a secluded forest, on a potentially dangerous mission. But not only that, she now knew the answers to so many of the secrets hidden in Michael's mind that she had wondered about for so long. She now knew exactly how he felt about her. She was no longer with Liam, no longer in relationship limbo.

This time, it was just her, Michael, and the forest with nothing standing in their way. This kiss was certainly different because neither of them had anything holding them back from one another. And neither of them knew exactly what tomorrow was going to bring.

Emma finally and reluctantly pulled away. Michael still had his eyes locked into hers as he spoke.

"Goodnight, Emma Walker," he said, his eyes reflecting his feelings.

"Goodnight, Michael Hale," she said, smiling warmly.

Emma headed into the tent, zipping it quickly behind her so mosquitos wouldn't follow her in and eat her alive. She laid down, listening to the sound of the wildlife around them singing what sounded like nature's lullaby.

With Michael just outside keeping watch, it wasn't long before she was sound asleep despite the hard ground beneath her.

Chapter Fourteen

The moment the sunlight came streaming through her eyelids, Emma launched up out of a deep sleep.

"Mandy," she thought, her heart racing.

Time was ticking.

Unzipping the tent, she peeked around the corner and saw Michael was already tacking up the horses.

"Hey Michael," Emma said, pulling the blankets and pillow out from the tent as she spoke.

"Good morning, I was just about to wake you," he said, smiling her way.

"Switch with me? You can probably take a tent down faster than I can," she said. Michael laughed at that.

"And you can probably tack up a horse faster than I can," he said, trading places with her.

Not even ten minutes later, they were ready to mount up and start searching the area for the cabin. Michael led the way on Manny and told Emma to keep her eyes peeled for any signs of the cabin, or the four-wheeler tracks that could lead them to it.

"Maybe we should split up and cover more ground?" Emma offered, getting more nervous as each minute passed.

"No way, I don't know what Clint is capable of or if he has any weapons. If you ran into him first without me there to protect you...," Michael didn't finish his sentence, he simply shook his head and seemed distraught by the thoughts that followed.

"Ok," was all she said. He had a point, but that didn't make her feel any better about how their time to find Mandy was running out.

They continued on at the walk, scanning every inch of the forest around them.

"Emma, freeze. Don't say anything, and ask Valentine to halt," Michael said, his voice low and soft. Something about the way he spoke scared her.

She looked around, finally seeing what had Michael worried.

A bear.

Emma tried to shove her panic down. What did she know about bears? They don't want to attack and want to be left alone. With grizzlies you played dead and with black bears you...froze? She supposed that made sense since that's what Michael told her to do.

"Valentine and Manny, please don't spook," she thought, forcing herself to take slow, quiet breaths despite her rising panic.

The bear stared back at them, unmoving, assessing them.

"No cubs," she thought. That was good at least.

Valentine snorted loudly, and Manny began to dance a little under saddle. The bear took one step in their direction, then two. Pausing to reassess them.

"We are going to back up the horses slowly," Michael said, his voice still low and eerily calm.

The bear watched them but didn't make another move forward. Emma was suddenly thankful for the fact that these horses had dressage training as they continued to back up.

Finally, the bear grew bored and walked off in the other direction. They stood there a moment longer, making sure it was long gone before moving on.

They headed the opposite direction of where the bear had gone just to be safe. They eventually circled back, covering ground they hadn't checked yet near where they had originally seen the bear.

"Michael!" Emma said, pointing at the ground.

He pulled Manny up to a halt, and his eyes followed her finger as he scanned the brush that appeared crushed with a divot in the ground clearly caused by tires.

"We got him," Michael said, his voice low and quiet now as he scanned the area. Emma looked around but still didn't see a cabin either.

"Let's go," he said under his breath as he led the way, following the tracks leading further into the forest.

They rode another five minutes before Michael suddenly halted in front of her, holding his hand up. Emma saw it at the same moment he did; a break in the trees which exposed a very old looking cabin. One that looked just like the picture Clint sent from his phone.

Michael dismounted as quietly as he could and handed Emma Manny's reins. Emma fought the urge to follow him. The only thing holding her back was the horses on either side of her who were safer far away from Clint.

Michael slid his backpack off and pulled a can of what looked like pepper spray out and handed it to her, his eyes conveying his worry.

"In case you need it," he whispered.

Emma nodded. She hoped she wouldn't need it.

He put the backpack back on and started walking towards the cabin. Emma caught his hand silently, and Michael stopped in his tracks and turned around.

Leaning in, she kissed him quickly.

"Be careful," she whispered.

Michael nodded and began walking back toward the cabin. Emma stood there, watching him disappear around the tree line, feeling helpless. She wasn't sure what was worse; standing here feeling helpless or being chased by Bo last year. At least when she was being chased, she felt like she had some power over her situation. Here, she was just waiting and hoping.

She wasn't sure how long she had been standing there. Five minutes maybe? Or was it ten? It felt like an eternity.

Her heart stopped for half a second when she saw Michael come through the tree line with Mandy at his side. He had one arm looped around her back making sure she didn't fall. She looked awful. Had she eaten? Or had water? Had he hurt her?

Suddenly, Michael paused, his eyes wide. In that same split-second Emma heard what he was seeing behind her: a four-wheeler. And it sounded like it was coming up on them fast.

Emma spun around, and watched as Clint tore through the brush, beelining for her. His eyes were filled with rage as he stared her down, his gaze flitting slightly at Mandy and Michael before landing back on her.

Emma looked at her horse for half a second, then back at Michael who was running full speed toward her. Mandy leaned against a tree, a look of fear was clear on her face as she stared back at Emma.

"Run!" Michael yelled, the four-wheeler seconds away. He knew he wasn't going to reach her before Clint did.

Run? Clint would catch her in a second! If Emma had learned anything it was that her horse had her back. Valentine had saved when Bo had chased her down and she would have her back this time too. But what about Manny? She could just let go of the reins, but he could hurt himself or spook and run off, and who knows how they would find him then. He could step on the reins and hurt himself too. Plus, the bear couldn't be that far off either.

"Sorry bud," Emma said to the gelding as she put one foot in the stirrup attached to the saddle on Valentine's back. She held on tight to Manny's reins as she spun her horse around, and luckily for her, he followed suit.

Emma bridged the reins connected to Valentine's bridle so she could steer her with one hand. Making a kissing sound and flapping the reins that she still held tightly, Emma signaled to Manny they were about to move. Valentine cantered off, and to her relief, Manny followed closely at her mare's side. They cantered into the deep forest, and Emma did her best to find the clearest path as they wound through the trees and foliage. This was far from the ideal ground to be chased down. She broke to a trot several times, cutting through tight spots when she could, and opening the horses' strides where possible.

Still, she could hear the four-wheeler close on their tails.

"I can't outrun him in here!" she thought, breaking back to a trot to weave around another thick set of trees. She was getting further away from the cabin and knew it was only a matter of time before she was lost out in these woods with someone who deeply despised her.

A very, very bad combination.

There was only one logical plan left. Emma brought the horses to a stop, dismounting quickly as she tied both horses' reins to a tree, jogging away from them.

Emma put her hands in the air and stood there as Clint quickly caught up with her.

He turned off the four-wheeler, and stood there staring at her, his eyes glazed over with rage.

"I'm sorry about your brother, Clint," Emma said, her hands still raised above her head. He said nothing but continued to stare her down as he got off the four-wheeler.

"I didn't know about your family, but I also didn't ask for this, or what Bo did to me," Emma said as calmly as she could, standing stalk still. If she was lucky, she could reason with the person hidden behind all that anger.

"You caused this! You made him do what he did! You ruined our lives!" Clint shouted, taking another step toward her.

"I didn't know, Clint. I'm sorry. You don't have to do this though. Just let us go home and go back to Alabama with the money we already deposited," Emma said, keeping her voice low.

"It's not enough! The bank is taking our house and it's all your fault! Give me the money and you can go," Clint said stepping closer to her again.

"There is no more money Clint. We tried, but we don't have that kind of money to…," Emma began.

"I know you have rich friends! You got that other money pretty fast; I know you're just holding out!" Clint said, moving forward with every sentence. He was only a couple steps away from her now, and Emma knew his anger was blinding him. He couldn't be reasoned with anymore.

Emma kept talking, planning her next move carefully. She only had one shot at this otherwise he could easily overtake her.

"Clint, why don't you tell me how much you need and maybe we can figure something out...," she said, her voice trembling a little bit this time. He was far too close for comfort.

"I need to take the money and start over! I need to...," Clint began saying.

"*Close enough,*" she thought.

Emma whipped the mace spray Michael had given her from her pocket with one swift motion, never taking her eyes off Clint. She took one step forward as she simultaneously sprayed it directly into his eyes, closing hers and stepping back the minute it made contact.

Clint screamed, his hands covering his eyes as he dropped to the ground.

Emma spun on her heels, running as fast as she could back toward the horses. Untying them, she quickly mounted up and ponied Manny behind her again, following the tracks that the four-wheeler made.

Emma cantered when she could, weaving through the trees again as her eyes followed the tracks leading her back toward the cabin.

"Emma!" Michael yelled, running towards her when she popped out from behind a wall of brush. He met her halfway, and she slid off Valentine and into his arms, tears rolling down her cheeks now.

"It's over," she whispered, more to herself than anyone else.

"Mandy!" she cried, turning to where she had been standing next to Michael.

"I'm ok," Mandy said weakly as Emma ran headlong towards her battered looking friend. Emma wrapped her arms around her friend as gently as she could.

"Are you ok?" Emma asked, looking her friend up and down.

"Do yourself a favor and never lay in the back of a pickup truck unconscious," Mandy said, a small smile breaking over her face. Clint may have highjacked her friend, but he certainly hadn't broken her sense of humor.

"Ladies, we need to get out of here," Michael warned, his eyes scanning the forest in the direction Emma had returned from.

Emma took the backpack from Michael and helped Mandy onto Manny's back, behind the saddle. She figured Mandy was safest with Michael and Manny. Mounting up on Valentine, Michael led the way back through the forest.

He took them a roundabout way which he said was a little longer, but it was out of the way enough that Clint wouldn't find them in case he decided to tear after them on the four-wheeler when the effects of the mace wore off.

Emma didn't care.

All that mattered was that everyone she loved was safe again.

"Sorry, Mandy," Emma said as Mandy winced when the cold ice pack touched her bruise. Mandy sat in a chair on the patio outside while Emma stood beside her.

"It's ok," Mandy replied, taking another sip of the margarita Emma made her in the house before attempting to ice down her injuries.

"All this really came from bouncing around in a truck bed?" Emma said, eyeing the scattered black and blue spots on her friend's arm.

"Yep. After that Clint had me tied up and I pretty much only saw him when he would stop by to bring me food and water once a day. At least he didn't starve me to death," Mandy said, rolling her eyes.

Emma knew her best friend was strong, but she never knew quite how strong until today.

"Did he even tell you who he was?" Emma asked curiously.

"Not really. He just mumbled a bunch of stuff about how they owed him for what they did. I tried asking him who, but he would just get mad and leave again," Mandy replied.

Michael walked across the lawn towards them, hanging up the phone moments before he reached the patio.

"That was the police calling us back. They found him," Michael said, sounding relieved.

"Thank God," Mandy said, taking another sip and wincing as Emma moved the ice pack to another bruise.

"Monica called, by the way. She said to take all the time you need coming back to work," Emma said, moving the ice pack again.

"Oh, I see you are on a first name basis with my boss now?" Mandy said, laughing a little while still wincing.

"Well, you know, people tend to bond over life and death situations," Emma replied sarcastically.

"Oh, and Cathy called a little bit ago too, she was asking how you were. Apparently she is sending us some sort of care package. She didn't say what's in it, but it's Cathy, so it's bound to be good," Emma added.

"I better be invited over when that arrives," Michael said, raising an eyebrow. He was no stranger to Cathy's elaborate gift giving.

It seemed strange to think that just this morning they had been scouring the forest for her missing best friend. Now here Mandy was, back like nothing had even happened. Well, besides being a little worse for wear that is.

Emma turned around at the sound of tires on the concrete and the metal gate opening. Emma and Michael exchanged confused looks. Neither of them was expecting anyone today. Maybe it was Clara? Or Lily coming to check in on them?

Turning her head, Emma's jaw dropped a little when she saw Liam's car park beside the house.

Emma shot a confused look at Michael.

"What is Liam doing here?" Mandy whispered, asking the same question they were both thinking. It wasn't as if Liam lived down the road.

Liam stepped out of his car, his eyes falling to Mandy's bruised up arm, then to Michael and finally to Emma.

"Sorry for just stopping by like this," Liam said, looking right at Emma. "Mandy, I hope you're doing ok. I'm so sorry to hear about what happened to you," he added, briefly glancing down at Mandy again.

"I'm fine, thanks," Mandy said, her eyes darting back and forth between Emma and Liam.

"Emma? Can we talk a minute in private please?" Liam asked, his voice not giving away what the conversation was about.

What could she say, no? He had driven almost four hours and she owed him an explanation, which is why she assumed he was here.

"I'll be right back," Emma said, meeting Michael's gaze briefly and handing Mandy the ice pack. Michael didn't say anything, only nodded. She tried not to stare at his worried expression too long.

Emma led the way into the house, sitting at the dining room table.

Liam stayed standing, looking concerned.

"I'm sorry Liam, I know our conversation on the phone was a poor way to end things between us. Especially with this being your aunt's farm and we will probably see each other in the future from time to time…," Emma began but stopped talking suddenly when Liam took her hand in his. His eyes locked into hers.

"Emma, I love you," Liam said, cutting her off before she could begin speaking again. Emma's jaw dropped and she clamored to find something to say. This was not how she expected the conversation to go.

"Liam, I…"

"Let me get this out, ok? Emma, I'm sorry. I put my work before our relationship. I could have done better to make the long-distance thing work. I should have done better. After we talked on the phone the other day, well, that was a wakeup call for me. What's the point in having a good job and a career if you can't share it with the woman you love? I did a lot of thinking and I want you back, Em," Liam said, dropping to his knees now.

"Liam…," Emma began again, but suddenly she didn't know what to say, because in front her was a tiny velvet black box open in front of her with a shiny diamond ring sitting inside. Emma gasped audibly; her jaw dropped again.

"I know long distance is hard, but I have an idea on how we can make that work. Move in with me. I bought a place in Wellington, and you can drive down and stay there on the weekends with me. I'll drive up here once a week and stay the night, and drive to work from here the next morning. Maybe down the road we can figure out a more permanent solution, but Emma, will you marry me?" Liam asked, his eyes still locked on hers.

Emma's own eyes were wide as she stared at the sparkling ring and then the pleading look on Liam's face.

No, this is definitely not the conversation she planned on having with Liam.

"I...I...need to think," Emma said, standing up suddenly.

Her heart felt like it had been torn in half. Here Liam was giving her exactly what she wanted and needed all those months they were together. Had he asked her this very same question a mere month ago, her answer may have been very different.

But so much had changed since then.

"*Michael,*" she thought, remembering the magical kiss they had shared on the front porch only a few feet from where they stood. That kiss had changed everything for her.

"*I need to get out of here!*" she thought.

Emma didn't think or look at Liam. Instead, she turned and headed down the hall to the staircase that led to the basement and ran out the back door where no one would see her.

Emma ran across the backside of the house and slipped through the empty space between the fence lining, running again once she hit the back road in front of the property.

Emma didn't stop running until she was out of breath, and at least a mile down the road, stopping to put her hands on her knees.

She walked over to the large oak growing next to a fence line where she collapsed against it, breathing hard still. Her mind raced, every possibility of what her future could look like based on this one decision flashed through her thoughts.

"What am I going to do?" Emma said out loud, choking up a little as she spoke.

Whatever decision she made would affect the rest of her life.

And making that decision was not something she was prepared to do today.

The End

(To be continued in the *Impelled Series* Book Three, *Red on the Right*).

Notes From The Author

Thank you to the readers who took a chance and read
my debut series. I hope you enjoyed reading it as much as I
loved writing it!

If you enjoyed it, please be sure to leave a review so others have
a chance to find it as well.

Reviews help me tremendously as an independently published author and it also helps other readers!

Sincerely,

Sarah Welk Baynum

Subscribe to my newsletter (sign up form on my website home page) to be the first to know about the release date for the next book in the *Impelled* series!

https://sarahwelkbaynumauthor.com/

About the Author

Sarah Welk Baynum has an extensive equestrian background which became the inspiration behind her debut novel "Impelled."

While writing her novels, Sarah draws from previous experience as a working student, show groom, barn manager, working for FarmVet and other various other jobs in the horse industry over the years both in her hometown and in Wellington & Ocala,

Florida. Sarah also attended Otterbein University and majored in Equine Business and Facility Management.

Sarah still owns horses and actively competes in show jumping and three-day eventing, and horses have been a big part of her life since the age of twelve. Her first horse may have been a gelding, but she has a bias towards mares and has primarily owned mares throughout the years.

Besides writing equestrian novels, Sarah also writes articles for Sidelines Magazine.

When she isn't writing or riding, Sarah also enjoys competing in local and national singing competitions, and mainly sings country music.

Today, Sarah lives in her hometown just outside of Columbus, Ohio, with her family which includes her husband, her two dogs, two cats and her two mares Tilly (a warmblood) and Letty (an off the track thoroughbred).